The Fate of the Foetus

I0683163

A Novel

Mohamed Gibril Sesay

Sierra Leonean Writers Series

The Fate of the Foetus

Copyright © 2017 by Mohamed Gibril Sesay
All rights reserved.

ISBN: 978-9988-8697-1-7

Sierra Leonean Writers Series

To my brother
BURHAN

CORNALUS

Big rain big rush everywhere to hurtle private dirt down public gutters, gutters that are munching streets having so many sore-like potholes, potholes that ooze mud-coloured pus, pus that are in turn carried by private feet unto private doorsteps… the cow who defecates on the street does not know it is only dirtying its own backside.

So the sky laughs so hard and long that its face glows with laughing wrinkles radiating downwards towards our community of Cornalus couching under the rotting tits of a chimerical lioness.

This is Cornalus where youths at junctions front-bite and backbite and tote burdens for the market women lashing obscenities at their sweating spines.

This surely is Cornalus for omolankay and men, bafpan and women, drays and boys, trays and girls and fowl and dog-poo and cassava leaves and dogs and rats and akriboto and arata and vultures and okobo and uniforms stripped, unstripped, and consecrated and and vomitus are all in a gyre of sole-licking for survival in the miry mort around Fort Thorton.

Yes, yes it is the city of the man who eats a thousand shine-pans of aborbor while onlookers defecate the millennium excreta in a single day on some filthy ground at the centre of the market that has not been swept for a whole jubilee.

This is the city where others survive the whole year on a butter-tin-cup of gari mixed with a tomato-tin-cup of pepper only drinking water to cool their burning insides.

This is the city of many tongues snakelike spitting poisonous words, and angel like cooling bruise souls.

In this space a friend knocks down a friend in the medicine-man's looking glass and every one attends the funeral of the woman who died giving birth to a krifi, which in English means spirit malevolent or benevolent.

But this is also the city of many who do not believe in this nonsense about the supernatural, such nonsense as wanfut jumpi, mami wata, underworld, next world, but many choose to keep quiet because they think it is not worth trying to prove this to the people of Cornalus.

This is Cornalus where people think to suffer and laugh to keep themselves away from thinking. Some say the community got its name from once being the corn field of one Pa Alusine, so people call it Corn Alusine which got shortened over time to Corn Alus. Others, especially the ruder younger ones say all that is nonsense. They say Cornalus is called thus because the loose skirts of women we call lappa are loosened in its dark corners - sometimes by the women themselves to pee, other times by mutual consent of lovers, sometimes by rapists; so many corners of looseness here.

Here we remember the future for as nothing changes the future is like the past and every person not laughing remembers that.

In this city no one breaks the law, they only break the pocket of law-patrollers sewing a thousand pockets every night.

This is where the curse - 'may God hammer the front-sides of those who don't want better days for us' - rends the night skies; or that 'may God make witches crash to death with their planes made of groundnut husks.'

In this esplanade everybody everyday celebrates living through yesterday and the very last hour.

Man jalaji man jalaji…

This is the city of daring witches who suck the blood of children even at noon.

Man jalaji man jalaji…

This is the city of stories more than the grains of sand in the whole world so no one can write them down even if the rancid plagiarist has all the trees for pens and all the oceans for ink and the energy of a quadrillion fusing nuclei.

Man jalaji man jalaji…

Fi sabilila fi sabilila…

Now look at them coming, mama papa children, one child behind one in front and all singing the begging refrain -

Man jalaji man jalaji…

White caftan now cassava-skin-coloured over papa's broomstick body.

Man jalaji man jalaji...

Road raped, unwanted foot pregnancies, perpetual miscarriages through the toes, bleeding soles oozing pus feast for the flies.

Man jalaji man jalaji.

Dignity-bare clothes starving on mama's famished soul.

Man jalaji man jalaji...

Ah, now mama is vomiting her guts falling down on the unshod dirt-damp children wailing and singing for compassion.

Man jalaji man jalaji man jalaji man jalaji fi sabilila wa lirasulila - who is he who is he who is he in the way of God and the Messenger of God?

But says a fanatic of better Arabic accents, don't give them a dime until they correctly pronounce the word and interpret them as well as this: man daladi ukridu llah karrdan hasanna - who is he that is ready to loan God a beautiful loan. Say that o beggars or you won't have a dime.

Papa tries to say it, but could not, mama tries but could not, children try but could not...

The real poor cannot master the proposal format. The real poor have poor accents.

Man jalaji man jalaji who is he who is he?

We are now at the famous junction of Cornalus and here comes this mad one scaring the children with his penis he dangles for money from the women singing around it obviously enjoying the disgrace of a promiscuous husband. They say he jilted a woman who had done so much for him; so the woman went to a medicine-man and got him mad.

Here comes this other one with a bundle on his head not knowing where he is going but surely knowing that where he comes from is on fire because all of them at that place are rivals now. In- laws date in-laws, friends date their friends' lovers, residents in the same house themselves, and more and more.

This is the junction of Cornalus fluffy warm as wing-pit of mother-hen, raw as gushing life, tragic-funny as brief vain struggle of an ill-tied ill-slaughtered goat.

Won't you salute the mirroring effects of the junction of Cornalus– its signs of despair and hope, blights and lights, eggs smashed, palm-oil poured, broken beans spilled by some jinxed person dawn-dreaming that this fane of false transience would …

This crisscross of gutters daily floods crisscross of soles and crams our hearts with the hunk and chunk, odds and ends, fits and feats of Cornalus. We hate it we love it – this miry earth on our house-steps opposite the unpainted school adjacent the unfinished house opposite the three bedroom moth eaten tottery structure housing forty three human beings and a million creepy-crawly mosquitoes, nits, ants, bugs, fleas, lice, rats and roaches.

This craze cross now tangles destinies, like twine round cock's foot, eating into flesh, tumescent, gangrene, growing rank, oozing pus foul as belch of a constipating dog.

This is the city of Osman, Wara, Sata, Lamin, Yembeh, Koth Yaro, Maimuna, Ya Sento, Kapay Jahanama, and a host of others, and it is to the telling of some part of their stories that we now turn.

OSMAN

When Pa Kaly went to ask Osman why he threw Wara out of his house, he met Osman sulking in the night of a foetal posture. Outside, it was not yet night, daytime light streaked across Osman's bowed back, head dangling between knees, fingers consoling toes. Pa Kaly coughed to draw attention. None. He greeted, but Osman was lost in himself. Pa Kaly moved towards him.

Osman was still fiddling with his toes, Pa Kaly stood over him, wondering how this warped young man would react to his words. He tapped his nape, "son..."

This startled Osman; he fumed, "it's no rumour, no rumour, I saw her myself."

Montages of another man on top of his darling daughter Wara flashed on Pa Kaly's heart-screen. Could it be Yembeh? No, Yembeh is dead, dead men don't make love. Nonetheless Pa Kaly blurted, "what son...did you see him... him on... ah... him him another man on top of..."

Osman did not see a scene as ugly as that. But how could he relay what he had experienced in a way that Pa Kaly would understand. Osman envisaged what he saw yesterday as upside down. But it was nonetheless real, as real as a cockroach on its back and fighting to regain its natural posture. It was this jostling of his knowledge to regain its natural veracity that hurt.

"Tell me son," Pa Kaly continued asking, "did your neighbours gather round, did they devour the sin like hogs devour filth at big wharf."

But the young Osman was not with the old Pa Kaly. Rather, he was devouring the bitter memorabilia of what he encountered only yesterday:

"Smile now, Wara," Osman said.

Wara replied, "Why are you doing this to me?" Wara's face was damp with tears.

"What… What did I do?" Osman asked.

Why did you marry me? Why did you push Yembeh away from me?

"Yembeh was foolish, unserious, hot-headed, he would have ruined your life."

"But that's what you are doing."

"I love you, Wara, more than myself."

"I'm going."

"Where?"

"I'm sick."

"Then we must see a doctor."

"I must see a doctor, not we."

"Well if that…"

"I want money."

"Look under the pillow."

8

She grasped her handbag, heaped money into it and flew out.

Osman plumped on the bed, his hands gesticulating like those of an ignorant fanatic petitioning his Lord "My God, my God, why has thou made me love one who does not love me?"

Suddenly, with a harrowing cry that surely tore the hymen of heaven, he pulled a shirt off the rack, which, too weak to withstand the jolt, fell, capsizing the water bucket on the groaning table. Hair unkempt, shirt unbuttoned, right foot unshod, he dashed out of a door dashing after him.

Bang! That was a taxi door dashing after Wara.

He yelped at the next cab. It stopped. Bang too!

"Are you crazy," the driver howled.

"After that red taxi, I'll pay, no problem, after that red car."

At the hospital, he saw her questioning a man. But it seemed as if the answer she got displeased her... for tears were gushing out of her already swollen eyes. He rushed towards her.

"What is wrong, dear?"

"Get out of my way."

He obeyed. She disappeared. He could not. His mind was as rumpled as a newly raped upon bed. The man Wara had been questioning came along and said to Osman, "please don't let her do it, everyday young women die here aborting their pregnancy."

"But I haven't touched her yet, I haven't touched her, I haven't touched her yet... Pa Kaly, I have not yet touched her."

9

This sudden vehemence startled Pa Kaly. "What son, what!"

"I never touched her, never, never, and now she is pregnant."

"What," Pa Kaly said, "my daughter is pregnant and you her husband has never touched her?"

WARA

Wara winced with shame as she walked through Cornalus. Her ejection from Osman's house hurt her. More so because she had not wanted to go there. Everybody saw her publicly reject Osman's calabash when Osman's people came to her house to ask for her hand in marriage.

"Take the calabash and give it to your father Pa Kaly!" The master of ceremonies had ordered her. She had not budged.

"Don't be shy, take it, it's for you!"

Very slowly, like an old woman genuflecting, she knelt in front of the calabash.

"Take it now!"

Her grief-clouded eyes let go their contents. Torrential tear-falls that no one now living had seen before poured down with a thundering cry, "No No I don't want Osman; Yembeh is the man I want."

The tear-falls hit the land with such vehemence that mud spluttered on the dignity of all. Her lamentations questioned the significance of marriage and parenthood and of everything that was within striking distance of her words. She lambasted the clergy for sanctifying loveless unions; elders for sweet-tonguing everyone into them... and she even cried against God for remaining silent when evil raged. "Did they not say silence means consent? To hell with everything, everyone."

Her father's rage knew no bounds. He was a whole storm in himself. But Wara had long learnt that her father's rage was like the beginning flurry of the bush fowl; it could not raise him to the top of her fears.

But that had not always been the case. His father's outbursts had once been devastating moments for her. Trembling moments. Until one day. One quiet day when she heard him groaning whilst defecating. The pit-latrine of their compound was poorly walled, and all sounds from there came out to the listening ears of many. So many of the elderly more respectable residents chose to do their bodily things in the dead of the night, when ears would be sleeping. But Wara's father had a running stomach that day, and he could not wait until nightfall. And Wara heard the sounds of the father. Just like her. Hmmmmm Hmmmmm. The groaning delighted her. She told her playmate Yembeh, and together they developed the habit of seating by the latrine to listen to grown-ups groaning.

In their hideout, Yembeh told her things. But what intrigued her most was Yembeh telling her that his father begged his mother for something in the dead of the night; that he would even make her ride him like a horse to get that thing.

"And what's that thing?" she asked.

"Rudeness," Yembeh answered, "so you don't know? Come let me teach you."

Their secret rudeness continued. And they discovered many secrets of adulthood. She took to making pictorial representations of these secrets in her exercise books. Became adept at it. It thrilled her. Dissolved the fear of the adults and of all authoritarian personalities. After all there were things that they begged for, after all they farted just like her, groaned just like her. And she could draw these things; own them. So much so that even when they were not at it, she could still watch them doing it in her exercise books. Sometimes she drew the pictures as she deemed fit; it was delightful making things as one felt. Watching the drawings, changing this there, redrawing that, adding this, offered her much freedom, much more laxity. And it was in one of these lax enjoyable moments that her father caught her. She was looking at the drawing of a male organ shooting to reach the sky, but the clouds were dark, and the pilot of the organ was very confused. Pa Kaly thundered, but his thundering did not terrify her. For she saw in them the same delightful groaning and grunting.

It was that childhood delight that dried her tears on the day she refused Osman's calabash. It was it that suddenly made her laugh when she beheld her father roaring death threats against her...and against her mother... No no no. She stopped laughing. The tearful response of her mother weakened her resolve. She did not want to see her mother suffer. But no; so much tears, so much fear. And then Sata… What Sata told her. Because of these she agreed to become Osman's wife. Another marriage ceremony was arranged. She took the calabash and gave it to her father.

WHAT SATA TOLD WARA

Wara, you yourself know that I never wanted Mr. Sahr. You know where my heart is. But I'm with Mr. Sahr. Do you know why? To please my father. I still believe that the wrath of a father is strong enough to destroy a daughter's life. Look at Maseray, look at what happened to her. She denied her father. Refused him. Disgraced him. But look at how her life ended, they had to rush her foul smelly corpse to a hastily dug grave. Thus I agreed to marry Mr. Sahr. But in my own way. Let me tell you, Yakuba is not his son. No. I don't want him. With all his money and houses and vehicles… Lamin has my heart, my insides, my womb, my everything. He's the only one worthy of fathering my child.

At Yakuba's outdooring, Mr. Sahr told the Imam to call him Chernor. But Lamin and I had decided in our own little way to call him Yakuba. I didn't argue with my husband. I didn't tell the Imam not to call him my child Chernor. Why should I? I knew in the depths of my heart that it is the name a mother calls her child that sticks. So in my lullabies I called him Yakuba, his nappies I called Yakuba's nappies, his clothes I called Yakuba's clothes. Everyday, everywhere Yakuba Yakuba Yakuba.

Everybody started calling him Yakuba...even Mr. Sahr. Do you know what his name is in the kindergarten register? Yakuba Chernor. Look, men are true fools, if a clairvoyant tells you to sacrifice a stupid thing, sacrifice a man. My husband said he loved the name; that it reminded him of an eclipse of the sun in his childhood days. Yakuba Chayro Yakuba Chayro...that was how they sang to return light unto the world...Yes the combined name, Yakuba Chernor was the price I had to pay to get society's respect and approval for my ways, to return some light unto my world. It's all give and take. Getting one's way needs patience and understanding. Lamin is at college studying, my husband's money shoving him up. Everything is all right with him. Fat scholarship from me... my husband's money. When he finishes his studies, I'll make a plan, a clever plan that will make even papa advice me to leave Mr. Sahr... Then will Lamin come forward. Papa will accept him. He would have become a tough man by then, one who a father would want for his daughter. Therefore Wara, don't be afraid of becoming Osman's wife. Look now, your mother has been kicked out of her matrimonial home because of you. Is that just? Must your mother suffer? No, Wara. I understand your dilemma; your heart is with Yembeh; you don's want Osman. But for your mother's respect and her marriage you should put up with him. You should, Wara. It takes time. Call

16

Yembeh. Tell him all this, he will understand. Tell him it is only for a while. No situation is ready made for anyone, no person is. But with skilful patience, like you are playing a game, everything will come out fine. It is hard for us, womanhood here is painful, you have surely heard that saying, every granny says that. But it's not your father who will be Osman's wife. It's you. And because it's you, you can do it your own way. Take your revenge in a careful quiet way; like I'm doing.

YEMBEH JOINS THE RESISTANCE

Yembeh could not bear the news of Wara getting married to Osman; he felt betrayed, shamed. He felt like nobody. He ran into the army to become somebody and... It was all over the radio, all over the place: PRIVATE YEMBEH MARO WAS KILLED IN ACTION AT...

With Yembeh dead, Wara felt empty, no strength, no resolve. That very night of the announcement of Yembeh's death, she kissed Osman. She went over the pillow barrier she had placed between them since their marriage and kissed him. Osman smiled. But his white teeth looked like a shroud in the dark of their room. Wara saw Yembeh, dead Yembeh emerged out of the teeth, crying, telling her how he loved her, but how she had broken his heart by marrying Osman. Fear gripped her. Something was pinning her to the bed. She kicked, she shouted, all in vain. Osman sensed the struggle. He took out something in some bottle his father, Pa Sorki had given him and doused her. She calmed down. He asked, "What's wrong darling?" he gently wiped her tears.

Wara asked him to stop consoling her. He stopped immediately. Some minutes, silence. "This is not a violent man," Wara said to herself. "Gentle being, what gentle handsomeness, a real husband." Respect for him welled

18

up in her heart. And she decided to abort Yembeh's child. There was no need for it. Yembeh was dead and she was accepting Osman for a husband. So she must not have this physical presence of Yembeh in her. She cried bitterly against this new feeling flooding her being. She choked, she was going under, drowning, but Osman caught her naked and with this swollen belly, and threw her out to the gossipy crowd of Cornalus.

MR. SAHR'S PARLOUR

Mr. Sahr's parlour has everything that a much travelled person of taste cares about; spaciousness, heavenly ventilation, Yoruba figurines, Italian murals, Moroccan calligraphy, totemic icons and that mix of colours that gives everything an air of simple cosmopolitanism. There are three sets of chairs, and each set sits apart in all respects: the French made velvety settee in a circle like they are making an offering of the glassy lioness and cubs shimmering in the gloaming; the Italian sculptured chairs in a square having at its centre down on the intricately carved mahogany flooring a rotating American made globe playing with the rainbow lights from the Egyptian chandelier overhead; and the third set crescent-like facing a crescent shaped cupboard festooned with state of the heart gold and silver filigree and ivory and wood carvings from Russia, Mali and China.

Mr. Sahr sits on his third set contemplating his piling-up - eleven houses: this one, three for his extended family, two on rent to international NGOs, four rented to diplomatic missions and the other one which houses Sahr Imports & Exports; fifty trucks; four cars; bank accounts in England, America and Switzerland. He smirks, taps his leg, "I'm safe, never again will hunger arrest me and my family."

20

That's the enemy - hunger - the inability to answer to the call of the stomach. He hadn't known what that meant when he was at college; then his stomach stood on other people's feet. But the soonest he graduated, these feet gave way, and his belly tumbled down the mire of the famished. Invisible fangs stung his guts, and his insides writhed like earthworm in salt. He howled. Viands out of bull-like mouths dropped his way. He looked elsewhere, he would leak no body's droppings to relieve the pain in his guts. For he had a dream, his screams were beams his country needed to catapult itself out of the slough of abject conscienceless-ness. He clung to this vision, this dream, this beam until…

Until his voice fragmented into bits smaller than cut and discarded toe-nails. Nay, worse, for his words lost all symbolisms - they were like motes in harmattan. Nay, weaker, for no one heard his moral protestations. His elders cursed him, younger brothers abused him, the community called him a fool - that man eats conscience, see how robust he is.

YA SENTO AND PA KALY

Pa Kaly returned home from Osman's place boiling over. He met his first wife, Ya Sento, mother of Wara, grinding groundnuts. "Bastard-dog," he thundered, "adulterous mother of an adulterous daughter.

Ya Sento raised her eyes off the grinding board, "what have I done again to…"

A hard slap across her face. Head between thighs. Hands over them. Torrents of blow fell on Ya Sento's exposed nape, shoulders and back…gbop gbup gbop. His muscles failed him, a lump of dry emotion blocked his trachea. He staggered to his room and collapsed on the bed.

Outside, in the mud, Ya Sento coiled, bleeding inside, "What should I do now? I have done my best, I have always done my best to please him. When my daughter refused to marry Osman, he flogged me very hard and threw out my things in the dead of the night. I begged my daughter to save my life. My life, my respect, my everything depends on him. Even if my people had taken me back, others would take that to cuss me. Yes, they would say I failed as a mother, without good children, as a wife, as a woman. My word would lose weight among my companions. I would lose weight. I begged my daughter, went down on my knees, flat on the stomach that carried her for nine months. She listened to me, God bless her. Tears in her eyes she listened to me. But now, now, what should I do? Osman has kicked her out. What should I do now? The ungrateful Osman who came here on his knees begging me to beg my daughter to marry him, bringing all sorts of foods and clothes and words has kicked my daughter out. Yes, after he has satisfied himself he kicked my daughter out. But Pa Kaly blames me, says I'm responsible for my daughter's behaviour. What should I do now? Stand up to him? The beatings, the abuses, as if I'm still a child. I'm tired of being treated like a child."

Bedroom: Tears strolled down Pa Kaly's crinkled jaws. Noise, too much noise inside him, "everywhere they pester my life, give us our share, our share, give us our share. But where will I get their share. My life is finished, finished, they will kill me now. My life's guarantee is gone, gone.

"Wara, Wara, Wara… do you know what I have gone through to save you from them, do you know? You are their share, you are what I should've given them long long ago. When it was their turn, they gave their children for us to devour. But I refused to give you, you were my only child then, my heart, how could I give away my heart? They say sorcerers destroy their hearts on being initiated. But I was a sorcerer with a heart. I could not give you away. They were furious. I fled on my

23

groundnut airplane. They chased me. A bullet caught my craft's behind, it slowed down. I was losing control. A bullet hit my hands. I lost control and the plane crashed upon the coconut tree-port. Pain upon pain I staggered home to my body.

"My groaning awakened your mother. She asked, "what's wrong?"

"I gasped, "go quick, go call Pa Sorki."

"When your mother came with him I groaned, "ah Pa Sorki, ah Pa Sorki, I…"

"Stop," Pa Sorki thundered. "Ya Sento, wait awhile for us outside…Pa Kaly, I know all. The wizards and witches would've killed you as you were staggering home to your body, but I stopped them… I stopped them, you were only trying to save my daughter-in-law."

"Daughter-in-law?" I was confused, so I asked him what he meant.

He explained, "your daughter Wara has a bright star and he who possesses her shall get some of her good fortune. I know you need protection from the sorcerers and I'm ready to provide that if you promise that you will let my son Osman marry your daughter."

Outside, Ya Sento still coiled, bleeding inside: "Pa Kaly called me a loose woman; he called me that. Me? Me? Me a prostitute? Look I come from a noble family. My ancestors were chiefs, warriors, marabout… Mama, am I a loose woman? Am I a prostitute. Well Papa,

Mama, your daughter is suffering. I will put an offering of rice on my bedside floor this night. Papa do not forsake me, Mama your daughter calls."

Bedroom: tears still rolled down Pa Kaly crinkled jaws: "My Daughter Wara I have suffered much for you. Wara I have these never ending pain on my arm because I tried to save you from their mouths.

"Daughter they sacked me at my workplace because of this arm, they said that a cleaner couldn't afford to have an arm that hurt every now and then. Daughter, I lived under the threat of death from the sorcerers because of you. Daughter, do you know what that means? It means fear, it means pain. All because of you. They had long sentenced you to death. That was why I watched over you so closely. I didn't want you to stray into their path. Sorcerers only get people who are careless about their little ways. I know, I was a sorcerer. They pass through your little carelessness into your life and scatter everything in it. They make the little carelessness so big that all kind of nonsense could enter your life. Wara, that was why I watched over you so closely. I was not trying to enslave you, far from it. I meant no harm. Marrying Osman was the only way you and I could be protected, the only way. No one would dare touch the daughter-in-law of Pa Sorki. But ah Wara, you disgraced me, you said I discontinued your schooling because I wanted to marry you off. Wara, that was not the case. It was to save you.

Let me tell you, I was an office cleaner and I saw what powerful men did to vulnerable working women, to women seeking work, to smart school girls. They laid them on the floor, on the office carpet. That was why I was sacked. No, the bad arm was only the paper reason. Everybody in the office knew that. I couldn't bring myself to cleaning the slippery fluids they left behind. No Wara, I couldn't bring myself to be ordered by my bosses' girlfriends, girls scarcely older than you. No daughter no no no. I hated their arrogance against elders, against their fathers. Look at that Maseray... Aaaaah! Look at what she did to her father when he visited her at her school. Ah ah ah! she denied him flat. "What me?" her father was surprised. "Yes you," Maseray had replied, "my father doesn't wear rags." No body told me, with my own two eyes I saw how the girl disgraced her father. That was what was burning away my heart when I came home and saw the drawings of male genitals and anuses in your school books. No, Wara I didn't remove you from school like that..."

SATA

The world, they say, is a place of so much lying, of making up stories to get things done. But sometimes things go awry, and the lie makes them hurt more. Like the false story of Yembeh's death that Sata paid thousands to get over the radio. She had done it to make Wara forget about Yembeh and allow Osman to impregnate her before the foolish Yembeh's return from the warfront.

But things didn't work out as she planned them. Women dreamed, men reaped apart; women proposed, dogs disposed, often leaving behind trails of turds, which could be very ugly, especially when hit by downpours of remorse. Things didn't turn out right because the foolish Yembeh had impregnated before running to the war. And Osman, finding this out at the hospital where Wara had gone to get an abortion threw her out of his house.

Osman had tearfully told her, "Sata, I must do it. They say married women don't give birth to bastards, but I will know the child is not mine... For all the love I have for Wara I will not accept that child - Yembeh's child? No, Sata, no....Thank you for all you've done, but please, please..."

What should she do now? Osman had opted out of Wara's pregnancy; Wara was suffering. Her father, Pa

Kaly, had forbidden Ya Sento from helping her, from teaching her the easier ways of pregnancy. "It's hard, Sata," Ya Sento cried, "hard for a mother to be prevented from visiting her pregnant daughter."

Sata, ever contemplating detours round problems asked the sobbing woman, "Ya Sento, does Pa Kaly go to the mosque for the evening prayers?"

"Yes."

"Well then, Ya Sento, that's the time to visit your daughter."

Yes, that was how she used to evade her father to visit Lamin. The soonest her prayerful father was off to the mosque for evening prayers she was off to Lamin. There're openings everywhere, just use your head, openings for freedom come from the most unlikely places.

But Ya Sento was caught. Wara was in pregnancy pangs and she had overstayed to give her these perennial words of hope - it will soon pass. But Pa Kaly, on a tip off from some rotten gossiper, caught her.

That very night, whilst her father was dragging her mother through the mud-ways of Cornalus, Wara gave birth to a baby whose resemblance to Yembeh in everything but sex and sins became the chewing stick with which people of Cornalus brushed their memories.

Birth refreshes memory, dead parents are often remembered by the presence (or even absence) of some traits of theirs in their offsprings. We're memory aids, enfleshed mementoes. Many wept when they beheld Wara's child; even those who were contemptuous of Yembeh's life...All wailed like they did when news of Yembeh's death hit the crumbling radius of Cornalus.

Death softens hate; it gives people an opportunity to water down the venoms in their assessments. Yembeh's death had done just that to the people of Cornalus, and many did elect to accentuate his better parts - his jovial fearlessness, his calling a spade a spade.

But death is also absence, and absence erodes memory - out of sight, out of... You know the anecdote. Birth is a reversion of that absence, a re-assertion of presence, of what we're wont to forget. Wara's child reminded Cornalus of Yembeh's life with them and his death somewhere else. Which in turn bobbled up memories of lost friends and cousins who once played with Yembeh in the sloughs of Cornalus. There was Laji, there was Tolo, Sorie, Brima, and many more. This war claimed them, chewed and spewed them all over people's memories, like chaff, broken, wreckages of the war's avariciousness. Wara's child is a pandora box of memories.

Yembeh's mother moaned for son, Wara wailed for her love, she could hardly muster enough laughter to breastfeed her child. The child's health deteriorated,

Wara's heart sank the more, she lost her mirth, the gleam in her eyes.

But Sata knew Yembeh didn't die. It was all just a part of a make believe, a manipulation. But why should she hide the truth when the lie hurt more? "I must undo some strands of this lie," she vowed quietly, "that Wara may get out of this unhappiness."

It was harmattan, windy, cold, souls were dreaming of warmth. So when Sata entreated Kapay Jahanama to get Yembeh transferred to town, Kapay Jahanama, wagging his legs unashamedly demanded sex. "It's harmattan, madam," he said, "we crave blankets with eyes."

She gave him what he demanded, for Wara, that she would return to her real way of living. Everybody has her way of living. She had wanted Wara to live in another way, with Osman, but she failed.

So it is, life is full of detours, many of which are lies, false-ways created by tired feet seeking ease and comfort. Most times, however, the detours are taken reflexively, individual footsteps aren't preplanned, they're not contemplated, they're not remembered - the toes just traipse or scamper through shrubs of least resistance, through toe-ways of least hurt. Rarely do we know where we detour, rarer still do we even know we're making a detour, creating a way round some hard hard reality. And that's the problem - the not-knowing - for we edge on into the fiction, into the convenience of lies.

So the guiding star recedes behind the horizon, and we lose forever the path of truth, righteousness, eternity.

MONTAGES IN OSMAN'S REMINESCE

Night. Osman could not sleep, nor wake up. Midnight. Jumbling montages on red-screen inside shut eyelids. On this red-screen of memory Osman was sitting with his father Pa Sorki when he heard a sweet voice - "a get di tamatis."

Warm something swirled his heart. He turned, and beheld the owner of the voice. It was Wara, a neighbourly girl in tatters toting a tray of tomato - "a get di tamatis."

A high fore-head, dark-glossy like honey spread on a clean clay plate; big eyes, wild as raining season stream; a great nose, finely cut, visibly dancing to the rhythm of her breath; and the thick firm lips, drawn like the commanding new moon of ramadan, gave her face a glow of graceful determination. "A get di tamatis."

His small eyes met her great eyes, wild eyes sweeping all on the shores of its vision. He gasped, her gaze choked him, filled his lungs, flooded his whole being with its overwhelming presence.

"If you're serious enough you will have her when you're old enough." He started. It was his father. "If you grow up strong I'll make her your wife. By God's grace, nothing will stop me making Wara your wife."

Sweet relief breezed into him. Until his father's voice, he had not known the cause and hope of his heart swirling - he wanted Wara for a friend, soulmate, and companion. And his father himself, Pa Sorki, doctor of secret arts, had promised him the fulfilment of his hope.

But now, he was ashamed of his hope. An intense loathing for his own heart struck his being. Despite all that he had done for Wara, she could not return his love. But this heart, this foolish heart still craved her.

Peppery cerebral indictment on heart-wounds - why this yearning, this craze, this longing for a person who hates you? He moaned, cried, painful mementoes of efforts poured on this leaking dream, like a man pouring buckets of water on a leaking drum, sure proof of his madness. Yes, in the eyes of his peers, especially so Yembeh, particularly so Lamin, he was that: a mad man, worthless as piss on a wash-yard floor.

THE BIG HEADED BOY

The late Maseray's pregnancy passed the nine months mark...ten months...eleven months...twenty months. Her tribulation raged within like waves vexed by the gravitational madness of the lunatic light. Doctors and nurses of the Clinic could not fathom what was for them a mystery. A medicine-man did. But telling Maseray and her husband Koth Yaro, Lamin's brother, was not part of his earthly destiny...

His was not to tell his clients about their child's head getting stuck at the birth-way - pain upon pain, Maseray flung her legs at opposite ends of the stained walls of the labour ward, cursing her husband for not sharing the pain with her, as he had done with the pleasure that was the source of this agony.

But an old woman did warn her, "Maseray, it's not good for a pregnant woman to bathe in the open spaces of the night."

She did not heed the advice. She was one of the post-moderns. Everything is a myth. Even herself.

"Well at least put charcoal in the water."

She laughed the old woman off. But the granny had hardly left when a krifi slicked through her unprotected vulva and merged its identity with that of the foetus.

Outside the labour ward, Koth Yaro's mother, also Lamin's mother, who loathed what she called the free life of her daughter-in-law was telling relatives, "let her gbenthineh, let her gbenthineh, let her confess her wrong doing."

"Mama", said Koth Yaro, Lamin's brother, "this has nothing to do nothing with gbethineh or superstition or such other nonsense; lets buy the medicines, let rely on the doctors." So he poured money on the nurses prescribing this and that.

The head still stuck.

"Let her gbenthineh," Koth Yaro's mother, also Lamin's mother, was truly convinced about her daughter-in-law's wrong doings, "if she doesn't do that she will not give birth."

"Oh no, " said Koth Yaro, Lamin's brother, " that's not so, she has nothing to confess; let's rely on science."

The head still stuck.

"Sure,' Koth Yaro's mother, also Lamin's thought, 'this Maseray must have been up to some games against my son. For how could she claim to be true to my son when she never bothered to get me hot water to bathe, to give me the meals choicest parts, to show me my meals with respect. No, she never knelt down to give me water, never waited on me while eating; always coming and going, coming and going… never bothered to say goodbye or tell me where she was going… And my son such a fool. But he was not like that before he married this woman... Sure this woman must have put the last little jot of her faeces in my son's food, she must have given my son the dirty water left from the laundering of her dirty public knickers. Yes, I refused to eat the food she had carelessly thrown at me as she hurried to only God knows where. How could I eat that? I'm not a dog. No. I'm her mother-in-law, the mother of her husband, my own true son. No other person gave birth to him for me, so she should respect me more than she does her husband, for if I hadn't given birth to Koth Yaro, would she have seen him? If I hadn't cared for him more than I cared for my own body... When Koth Yaro came he asked me why I hadn't eaten. "Look Koth Yaro," I said, "I'm not a dog who gladly eats meals thrown at it." "She threw the food at you?" Koth Yaro asked. "Ask her," I replied. "Where is she?" Koth Yaro asked. "Eee Koth Yaro,." I shouted, "so you don't know where your wife is?" "I was not in when she went out... May be she had gone to..." "Hmm son who married whom?" "Why mama," Koth Yaro replied, "we married ourselves."

The head was slowly tearing its way through the birth-way. A nurse, no gloves, was impatiently trying to open Maseray with one hand and gyrating her backside with the other.

"Bring forty thousand," a nurse ordered the impatient Koth Yaro, Lamin's brother.

"Here."

She grabbed it like armed robbers do, went into a room, hurriedly came out with a dark bottle containing nothing, passed the mixed-up down Koth Yaro, Lamin's brother, and went into the suffer-ward.

"You married yourselves? Well done son… But who… who is the boss here… I mean who controls this house?" "Eee Mama, what type of question is that?" "I want to know, I really want to know…your wife is too free…too out of control…look Koth Yaro, if you want your woman to be faithful to you, be hard, that's what women look for in men."

The head reached the edge of the birth-way. But a rough scar at the upper end of the gateway to the world was blocking its final thrust to a new mode of existence. Time was running out… the near invincible accomplices of the medicine-man had foreseen the child being born before the mid-afternoon prayers… And at yonder mosque the muezzin was climbing up the minaret.

It was then that Yeanor invaded Koth Yaro's memory. He heard Yeanor saying this: "I told you, Koth Yaro, that you will pay for it, that I'll make you know that I haven't forgotten my roots."

"But Yeanor, Yeanor please," Koth Yaro, Lamin's brother, gasped after the shadow and bumped into his mother.

"What's wrong with you Koth Yaro?"

"She was here, I saw her."

"Who?"

"Yeanor."

"Yeanor, yes Yeanor… the real daughter-in-law that Koth Yaro kicked out for this false one. Ah Koth Yaro, you wronged Yeanor. You destroyed her schooling; you impregnated her out of school. But no, you never looked back to that… You kicked her out for Maseray. You met this wayward Maseray in a rum-bar, brought her home and ordered Yeanor out of the matrimonial bed. Yeanor refused. So you beat her up. You and newfound love Maseray, you beat her up…"

The muezzin was calling the faithful unto the mid-afternoon prayer. The head was getting desperate… It must get out during this time; that was what the medicine-man said…

Next to the writhing Maseray, another woman was giving successful birth to another boy for whom this as yet unborn child tearing the insides of her mother would be severely beaten for predicting:

"Eighteen years hence, you will strip your mother naked and stab her belly-bottom and then give your father the severest of beatings. And when the trial judge shall ask you why, you will reply, "mother disgraced me by sleeping with politicians to feed and clothe the family and for silently bowing his head to that, I could've killed father had neighbours not overpowered me."

But that was not the only time the prescience of this krifi-child landed him in trouble.

The other time he was flogged by inmates of a house he had predicted would be ablaze in about a month's time.

Ah, you remember the other time he told us about the approach of difficult times for the nation? Times that would be rougher than where chickens sleep... times when the pregnant would give premature birth on the fleeing road; when beasts shall devour the ill-born and the ill dead; about how three minutes old mothers would be raped by hard hearted men with guns; about barbaric slaughtering and kidnappings and savage butchering... about how even the blind would toddle on stones and swamps in blind dreams of safety...and about how even words would die from the fatigue of carrying more sorrowing accounts than they were made for...

And about that seaman he said water would kill. The man stopped going to sea... But then he choked on a teaspoon of water and died.

The children loved him. Not so the adults. The krifi-child frightened them with his hidden knowledge. He told them about themselves in public... joined those stories which they would want to keep apart... presented the fullness of their inherent contradiction in public. About what they did under the cloak of God under the cover of night. And especially so the greedy, the stingy, the rock-hearted, those who would not give him money to give his little friends.. These he told only the evil sides of their past, present and future. About how they slept with their sisters-in-law and ate monies meant for the building of the house of God. About how they would continue sleeping with their brothers-in-law. About the fangay they killed their friends with. About their envy, their bad heart, their dry eyes, their evil machinations against the successful; and about how they hid from their children to eat.

"Give money, give me money that I may give my friends, my hungry friends…" And the children would sing aloud:

> Big headed friend
> Big headed friend
> Big headed child with a heart
> Bigger than the world

And the adults would kick the little ones; stifle their sweet innocent voices. And the big headed one would coax them with memories of happier future times. When hearts would be sunny, when the world would care for its children, when children shall no longer be mercilessly flogged for worthless offences, when adults shall no longer eat the meat and give them the bones, when their privates, hearts, palms and tongues shall no longer be hacked off to make evil medicine for evil politicians, when they shall no longer be ill-fed, ill-clothed and ill-sheltered, when childhood shall indeed be the gardens that even adult would love creating for themselves, when there shall be no cholera, no diarrhoea, no kwashiorkor, no body hot as hell, no moaning in great dolour.

Thus the good children wept and the bad adults rejoiced when the big headed child was eaten up by a mangy cat whose head alone was twice its size.

"It's good that he should die this way... this child always has evil words in his mouth," the old man said.

"But he's laughing, enjoying it," the old woman added.

"Yes, he enjoys evil things even if they are happening to him."

THE FATE OF THE FOETUS: CONFESSIONS OF THE BIG HEADED BOY

One hot night, I was looking for a way to become partly human when I found Maseray washing in the open spaces of the night and zoomed into her unprotected vulva. It was good that I did; for the foetus inside Maseray was already disintegrating, already sliding down the path its other half came. Had I not given it stickiness, that foetus could have become a casualty of Maseray's uterine flux.

Casualties never end, only reminisces make them bearable. But even remembering is an art; you've got to have the flair for remembering things in sweeter and insightful ways, or else your memory becomes the tumbrel that carries you to the ultimate agony.

Casualties never end... Whilst potential humans were swinging from one rope to another inside the scrotums of matured human males, many actual human beings were in this world, swinging from one event to another...

Casualties never end; but the way you reminisce makes them bearable, even pleasurable. Some of the potential human beings never made it out of the scrotum, there were so weak that the aroused ecstasy of their fathers

42

could not swing them out of the nether sac; casualties of the struggle of life, for life… won't you hallow them?

Others got out but not in, they could not slide up the path towards their mother's wombs. They become filth that the mother washes off after sex. They leave no memory behind - without skeleton, they never had the chance to become fossils after been washed away in their mothers' Noah-like cleansing floods.   Lost forever? Perhaps.

Only dinosaurs leave fossils, only tyrants leave records for fine treatment at the museums of this and that history. That we may tremble.   But what about the vegetations the dinosaurs trampled upon, crushed. Well the scientists tell us the grass rot down there, eons later the vegetations become dark oil sucked up to lubricate this world, crushed in life and death.

Billions of events sprout out of every arousal of the world, but the vast majority never makes it to the memories of humankind. Why?

We cannot remember everything; it will be burdensome, too heavy to carry. So we select, so we let some stories die that others may live. Casualties never end, that we may be, they were wiped out. That our stories may exist, other stories were wiped out.

Every now and now billions of sperm race to hook up with ovaries and become human foetuses. But most times, only one spermatozoon gets into an ovum…

43

Nuances! Nuances! Nuances! Sometimes two spermato-zoon simultaneously enter two ova and we have non-identical zygotes. For the unsuccessful billions of spermatozoa, the result is always the same: the emergent zygote(s) play(s) the victor and through secretion of chemical repellents scare(s) off the unsuccessful desperadoes. What else, they've lost their chance to become higher possibilities for human existence. Millennia old genetic memories lost, eons old efforts poured on a hope whose realisation eludes them at the crucial moment. So they beat off a retreat (the story of their efforts imprinted in their disintegration). And they are cleansed off by the mother. The struggle continues.

Nuances! Nuances! Sometimes this victor, this mingling, this murderous zygote regrets being alone. So it divides into two and we have identical zygotes. Perchance if one fails to make it to the human realm, the other will.

Nuances never end! Sometimes the division is incomplete... Or two zygotes hug each other, they fuse their wee essences (or one tries to swallow the other, but the other resists; one cannot swallow; the other cannot be swallowed). They are given birth to thus, joined together at the head, chest or other parts, thorns pricking our will to definitional clarity; fuzzy; human-krifi with two heads and eight arms. Casualties never end for we kill them off.

Everyone of you is but a lucky actualisation of a possibility that contended with a million other possibilities each of which could have been actualised in the space and time you now occupy. Won't you say thanks? But to whom? Some say God, some say luck, some say other stuff that add to the division of humans.

Nuances! Nuances! Sometimes some genes run berserk; so unruly, they play not by the rules of the code. And behold another imperfection is groomed for the human realm. But who has not got nuances within? Or Without? Who is the perfect human in all their genes and traits and stories? Who? Who Who?

But too many nuances wrecked too many zygotes. Many foetus never made it to full term, too slippery they would not glue themselves to the warm tender sustenance of the uterus. Others hang on unto the fallopian tubes; they become ectopic pregnancies, endangering the lives of their mothers. But so many foetuses could not take a stand - lacking stickiness, they could not continue with the carriage of life, they become miscarriages. So unlucky, so unlucky.

That could have been the fate of the foetus that was in Maseray. But I energised it, I gave it stickiness, the will to resist the uterine flux, the will to hope for higher state of existence…

No, I didn't kill my human mother. I am not guilty of the accusation that I killed Maseray. Perhaps that scar did, that scar of the excision. The old woman said they did not do it to her in a bush, but in a room just vacated by mere boys, their impure smells that hurt still hanging about the place. She said Maseray was only there for a week! She said the ceremonies were all a mockery. The sore did not receive inner healing. They only tortured her flesh. She learnt nothing there. The old woman also said female circumcision is now meaningless. The scarifications lost their relevance as that which should continually remind one of what one learnt in Bundo. Nothing was learnt, so there is nothing to be reminded of. Nothing, nothing. The scar had no meaning, so it couldn't defend itself against the push of a very big head that was desperate to get to the human dimension of existence.

But people blamed the big headed boy. No naming ceremonies were performed to welcome me. No name was given to me save that which I gave myself. The world hated me for something that was not my fault. They treated me evilly, called him an evil spirit.

But that I was not. I was a messenger from the other side of existence. I had come to remind your people that unless they remember their other-sides, unless they remember the ancient lore of African spiritualities and perform ceremonies of recognition, we are all doomed...all doomed.

But my own human-father, Koth Yaro, said all was nonsense, that all were lies, that what I had was hydrocephaly - too much water in the head.

Those who believed otherwise did believe I was indeed a spirit, but that I was an evil one. They said I blinded Pa Sorki because he tried to make me return to the krifi-world. No, I didn't. I was ready to go. Why? Pa Sorki had already performed the honourable ceremonies that must be accorded us before we exit your dimension of being. He was someone who recognised me, who was performing a ceremony for me. Perhaps acknowledging his recognition of me would awaken the desire in him and you to continue with ceremonies of recognition, with oblation to us. So I ate the the rice-flour, swallowed the egg, lapped the palm-oil and I had already began entering my snake-skin tunnel to our dimension of existence when I felt the evil gazes of a man hitting my being, striking my fragile metamorphosing self in the vital parts. I had no choice to strike out his eyes to defend myself. If I had not done that, I would have become a bleak hole; I would have imploded into a bizarre state-of-intense-grief that-emits-no-radiance...

Many such blew holes abound now in the universe; victims of those who exalts difference, who don't like our freedom to choose the existence of our calling.

My friend, these people are now on the ascendancy; they destroy tunnels, they build walls. Hypocrites, whilst or after building the walls they lure us with dazzling ceremonies of affirmation of freedom into betraying the wherewithal of our snake-skin tunnels of freedom. Which they then destroy, shrinking into intense-existential-griefs-that-emit-no-radiance many of the beings that had wanted to become the marvellous existences of their imagination...

Be wary friend, beware, the universe has become less free now. The presence of intense griefs, which your astrophysicists call black-holes is limiting the playing ground of joyful existences. Danger, danger is everywhere, dangers not foreseen. These bleak holes out of which no radiance escape are dangerous. They implode into their intense sorrowing any existence that stray near them. I've seen many friends shrinking thus... You would be playing with them in a familiar place and just like that, just like that they implode... So horrible... How frightening is such a betrayal of the locus of an intense grief... How agonising is that awareness which comes by the lambent howling of a dear one being swallowed by a bleak hole... How traumatic to know that your own friend has gone into the intensification of something that may spell your end as a being of marvellous potentials... That's it my friend, even the spaces of the imagination are filled with them... even so the familiar spaces of your own endeavours

MAIMUNA'S AMULET

Maimuma: Lamin, you have a spirit-guardian...he hates our love for each other.

Lamin: Me? I have what

Maimuna: Yes, you, you have a krifi

Lamin: I don't believe in spirits, I don't believe in strange creatures that I can't see

Maimuna: Me too, until I was told my story

Lamin: Which story?

Maimuna: Mine, it all began in a dream... I saw my father making love to me…. Every night for forty days.

Lamin: Your own father?

Maimuna: Yes, one morning, I saw blood all over my thighs, I had been deflowered in my sleep.

Lamin: You must be joking

Maimuna: Ah no, it is not a joke. You see this amulet around my waist?

(Maimuna takes off her gown and allows her skirt to drop. A black chemise is exposed, and just above her hips, there is a a a brown leather-rope strung with cowries shells and multi-coloured beads.)

Lamin: Yes.

Maimuna: It is to ward off my spirit-lover, the rapist in my dreams that comes in the guise of my father… but it

49

took quite some time before we came by the medicine-man who....

Lamin: I'm going

Maimuna: Where?

Lamin: Out of this story, this nightmare, out of you

Maimuna: You can't...he who has gone into me is impotent before every other woman except me...yes as long as this....the krifi-lover knows that...that's what keeps him away from me.

(Lamin makes for the door; Maimuna blocks him.)

Maimuna: Lamin, I love you.....I love you for something you don't know

Lamin: What's it?

Maimuna: My krifi-lover cannot harm you

Lamin: Of course, that which does not exist cannot harm me

Maimuna: He cannot harm you, Lamin, the only human-lover in my life that he dare not harm. He killed Sorie my first love, then made Yapo mad... But you, he dare not harm you.

Lamin: Hmmmm.

Maimuna: He is afraid of the repercussion, your krifi will hurt him too.

Lamin: You are mad

Maimuna: I know

Lamin: And because you know, you will never get sane

Maimuna: I don't want to get sane… Sanity is slavery, extreme slavery… To be sane is to live a dull life

Lamin: Now this cord around your waist, won't you throw it away?

Maimuna: How can I throw away protection.

Lamin: You worship the cord?

Maimuna: Hahahaha

Lamin: I want to tell you one thing.

Maimuna: Say!

Lamina: That cord can't make me impotent. If I can go into you, I can go into any other woman.

Maimuna: You hate my amulet eh?

Lamin: It's a useless string of cowries shells and fanciful beads.

Maimuna: Say you don't have eyes for them… You have no faith, so you cannot see the whole picture of its relevance.

Lamin: I have faith in that which works, that which produces results.

Maimuna: Me too Lamin, this amulet has produced results… I no longer have those nightmares of a father raping me.

Lamin: Maimuna are you alright, do you know what you are saying

Maimuna: I have experienced worse times, the amulet works.

Lamin: So the truth is that which works?

Maimuna: Even lies work. But what is a lie? Is it not said that when a person says something is a lie, it is most likely to be something he does not believe in. Is that not so? Is that not so?

Lamin: You are a woman, don't shout like that

Maimuna: I should talk low eh... slow and low eh... like em em how your mother talks to your father....em em Kotho, your rice.... Em Kotho, water... eh...
Is that what you want... sure that's what your God decrees.

Lamin: Maimuna, do you believe God?

Maimuna: I believe in a God that's nobody's prisoner... a God not caged in by any-body's definition. My God is not blonde and nor does he only communicate in brown man's language. And my God is not the male so beloved by the priesthood.

Lamin: If your father knows about this, he will definitely disown you.

Maimuna: Do you know him?

Lamin: Everybody around this place knows your father... he is....

Maimuna: Will his knowing about my views unmake me?

Lamin: What?

Maimuna: My father disowning me

Lamin: Yes, disfigure you... pull off some strands of the web that is you....somehow unmake you.

Maimuna: God bless you for your advice, I will not make him know.

Lamin: Are you afraid?

Maimuna: No… He loves me very much… that would bring him much pain… much pain because he would think I will go to hell, the place of torment religious leaders say those who say things other than their definitions of God would go… you know my father is a member of the priesthood.

Lamin: Which means he too participates in that bizarre ceremony.

Maimuna: Some of the time, yes…. But at other times he rebels against it and sees God as an energetic ideal lifting everyone to the blissful space of the ideal….

That my father is a bizarre creature, a mix of things pleasant and unpleasant.

Lamin: And your mother, would she cry if……

Maimuna: She is dead….. they told me I was suckling her breast when she passed away… Ignorant infant me, they had…..

Lamin: Nooo….

Maimuna: That was what they told me…. She never recovered from our births.

Lamin: Your births?

(Silence. Maimuna sobs)

Lamin: (Withdrawing a kerchief to dry her tears) I'm sorry.

Maimuna: No.

Lamin is transfixed, his kerchief dangling in the air

Pause.

Maimuna: Kerchiefs don't dry tears

Lamin: (Putting his hand down) I'm sorry

Maimuna: You did nothing wrong... and I did not cry for pity.... Only that certain Stories come with tears... I was the last of a triplet that my mother gave birth to before she died.... My mother had buried three daughters and two sons before our births. Her co-wives accused her of being a witch, of eating her own children. That failed to convince my father. But when my triplet brother and sister were born dead, my stepmothers' wailing for their safety and that of their children pushed my father into sending my mother away. Disgracefully... spittle, dirt and ash all over her, ears deafened by that would make night fall at noon, tears on her swollen eyes, cane marks all over her, pelvis still weak, blood dripping down her thighs, my mother fainted on the threshold of her family dwellings.

Lamin: Babaric folks, woe upon them... superstition, terrible lies.

Maimuna: Yes, for that very night, an old woman...next door neighbour to my father had a dream... A little baby girl was telling her that she was about to be born to Alfa Sheku Maro and that she should go tell him that in order that this baby-girl may grow into a woman, she must be called Maimuna. The woman did not deliver the message, she did not take the dream seriously.

So Maimuna appeared to her in yet another dream, "look", she told her "if you do not deliver what I told you and I'm given a name that cannot steady me, that cannot make me live and grow in the human world, know that I will not die alone, but with you." That settled it. Very early the next morning, just after the morning prayers, the old woman Ya Posseh, scurried to my father with the message. Father was surprised, "No, I don't have a pregnant wife, the one that was pregnant delivered still born babies three days ago". But he had scarcely finished what he was saying when news came from my mother's family that mother had given birth to a bouncing girl... That was me, my dear Lamin.

Lamin: This is a heavy story, a very heavy story

Maimuna: Yes, a heavy story; that's why I'm Maimuna; that's why my father so cares about me, that's why I'm in college, that's why I love you, that's why I have this amulet, that's why I must not be circumcised.

Lamin: What?

Maimuna: Yes it's a taboo, against the medicine in this amulet... would make me lose my balance... against me

Maimuna turns away...Silence...silence loud with emotions...silences...so thick...like wet wood burning...

Maimuna bursts into tears, long soft soughs interspersed with sorrowful gasps... Lamin does not know how to react. He too is overwhelmed. Feels it. But he simply does not know how to express it in a way that will not earn him a rebuff... 'kerchiefs don't dry tears'...he still has that on his confused mind. Maimuna gasps "Lamin Lamin Lamin"...

Curving his arms as in a hesitant embrace, his emotions triumphant over inhibiting memories, over-whelmed by the desire to dance the practiced rituals of manhood - the desire to save a belle from drowning in a stormy sea of inexplainable emotions - Lamin runs towards her. But Maimuna's 'No No No' freezes his steps... 'Lamin Lamin Lamin' unfreezes them again. Too late. Clutching the insides of her thighs she slumps headlong into the savage crevices of the clammy floor...

Lamin meets her there, raises her head... opens her right eyelid with his little finger. He lifts her and gently puts her on the bed... gives her some milk... pours some water over her... It works... Maimuna opens her eyes and raises her head.... Slowly... slowly... Lamin helps her sit on the bed... Silence... Silence.... Like the fearful quietude that precedes authentic revelation.

Maimuna: Lamin...I always have this feeling...about the worse coming to pass... You see, I love bundo...the urge to break the taboo is very strong... I love the drumming of bundo... the beats... the songs... they make me happy…But I know I must not be circumcised…so anytime I hear the drumming, two opposing feelings would bobble up within me… feeling of joy and sadness…Mixing… sharp unfeeling things against my tendermost parts…so traumatic… But God! I love the drumming, the dance, the songs, the chalk-white gbonka. It gives me a feel beyond myself… something joyous… Thus I felt myself singing, dancing into the bundo bush…. But just as I was about to enter, I had sharp cries of pain within the joyous rhythms… painful shrieks mixing with the ecstatic songs… I wavered… stopped…. Turned around to… too Late… from nowhere, women, their breasts beating their bellies, all led by my maternal aunts, converged upon me… I fought back… they held me tight….pushed me into the bush, stripped me naked and clammed for my private parts.

Lamin: But that's only a feeling

Maimuna: Yes Lamin, but it's a feeling I feel will happen.

MAIMUNA'S LETTER

Dear Lamin,

You said I'm no longer with you most of the time, you said I've lately been moving around with so many guys. Now Lamin read this sympathetically, cooperatively you would understand me better.

Lamin, what should not happen has happened. I have been circumcised.

My maternal Aunt tricked us, father and I. They said they wanted me to spend the holidays with them. "Look Pa Maro," they said, "a child on the father side is a child on the mother side. Let Maimuna come spend the holidays with us."

Right words, too weighty to be cast aside like that. So father asked for my approval. Perhaps he was hoping that I would refuse. But I was anxious to be with my mother's family. But I had barely settled down in the village when they whisked me off to the circumcision grove. It was a hard fight, I knew I shouldn't be circumcised, you know why. It's taboo to the amulet; I would lose my balance. So I fought hard, but two women sat on my chest, a third on my belly and scores held my feet. In the scuffle the sowei cut more than she should.

58

It was a truly excruciating experience. Do you think it is for nothing when women say even if it were possible no women could love a second circumcision… But they love to see it done to others, a relay, passing on the baton of pain, a moment for the wildest celebration for the veterans of this gruelling race. My aunts said they did it for my mother; that she too could jump for joy among the silent spectators.

I cried throughout, my aunts coaxed me, sang to me, reasoned out their actions to me, told me things.

"Look, Maimuna, your father hates you, he doesn't want you to become a woman. Have we not told you how he ill-treated your mother? Don't you see what he's doing now, he wants you to go astray, to die. With that thing on you, would become a stray woman, you will run after men to satisfy your cravings. This is only to save you. We have done a lot, spent a lot. They fined us heavily for not finding you a virgin. You could have been treated badly, but we gave the sowei money, huge sums."

"I don't want to know," I cried out, "you've destroyed me, destroyed me."

"Look Maimuna'" my eldest aunt replied, "it's not good for a woman to be rude, men run away from ever-protesting women. You must bear your lot with dignity, with calm courage. We've all suffered, womanhood is painful, we've all passed through this, but we didn't shout out our pain as you are doing. It makes you ugly, women who shout are ugly Amy, tell her the rest."

"Maimuna, you have long passed the circumcision age. We tried a number of times to get your father's permission to circumcise you to no avail He said it was none of our business. He was right, he and your little mothers should decide when you should be circumcised. But when your stepsisters were circumcised without you, we decided that enough was enough. A child on the father side is also a child on the mother side, the indignity of an uncircumcised daughter is as much a shame on the mother side as it is on the father side."

"Maimuna," another aunt cut in, "we've suffered a lot on your account. All through this going and coming your dead mother has been blaming us for this, pinning us to our beds, flogging us in lonely paths, putting sand in our soup, splashing mud on our laundry. We couldn't stop her. No alfa could. It was just for her for pester us to circumcise her only daughter."

"Especially so after your sisters were circumcised. I saw your mother in a dream, she was weeping, saying that we've done nothing to stop your father and step-mothers from destroying you."

"Yes, Maimuna, where do you think we got all this money to get a good initiation for you, an initiation where no one dare whip you, where no one dare say any harsh things to you… eh Mailman where? You do not know? I'll tell you, from your mother, from your dead mother. We told her we are poor, that the country is as hard as stone, that we couldn't raise up the money to meet the ever increasing cost of circumcision. But she told us not to worry, told us to carry on."

"Yes, Maimuna, that's very true, one day a woman came along with very big boxes to Tha Bura. She told her a woman called Gbowara had given her the boxes. Yes, your own very mother, for your immediate circumcision. We had no choice, an ultimatum from the dead shouldn't be taken lightly."

"Yes Maimuna, what Kama has just told you was what happened. A woman, short plump one about Amy's height gave me the boxes and disappeared before I could ask her further questions about your mother Gbowara. Later that evening, with all my amulets about me, I opened the box. Ah Maimuna! You will see for yourself, just be patient till the day you become a shayma."

Lamin Lamin Lamin I wish you were there when I came out of the Bundo Society… Great cloths, music everywhere! Food aplenty! What is food! We forgot about death and immersed ourselves in the greatest festivity ever held in that village.

But Lamin, it was all a façade, a masking of what circumcision really is: bloody perpetuation of innocence of sexual pleasures. In my case, however, they got it wrong. I already knew, I had already tasted the forbidden fruits before they flayed the taste buds... So circumcision became like trying to make me revert to innocence, to calm boring innocence of my God given sexuality. But it's impossible, my memory guards against my reversion to pristine innocence. So when I couldn't get the pleasures in my first try after circumcision, I knew something was wrong. I tried again, nothing. Again; nothing. So I stopped being faithful to you .

Lamin. I pray you understand.

Me, Maimuna

THE SEPARATION OF LAMIN AND MAIMUNA

Lamin was aghast. Could it be that Maimuna was right, that her amulet would make him impotent before all but her? With Maimuna, he was potent, not so with his other love, Sata. Could it be that Maimuna was speaking the truth? Perhaps. She said that he had a krifi. And since that time he had been dreaming about the big-headed boy saying loudly to him that he was his guardian spirit. Could all this be his imagination playing havoc in his dreams? Dreams! The imagination actualising itself within fictitious esplanades within. But his impotence before all but Maimuna was all too real.

He was experiencing a bizarre change within; his faith in the world as it appeared to his eyes was changing. Was the world deeper than it appeared?

He was pondering over this when he received Maimuna's letter. He read it over and over again. The changes within became more profound. He was confused, and annoyed, and jealous, especially as he read on and got to the point where Maimuna wrote that she had stopped being faithful to him. He ran to Maimuna's room, knocked hard on the door.

"Maimuna, Maimuna, why are you unfaithful to me?"

"'You're jealous eh?"

"Going about sleeping with all these men won't bring you joy."

"You may be right… I'm now in a gasping sphere, in a limbo…. Searching for an experience I may never get again."

"Well stop going after men, it's immoral; worse, your amulet is making our best men impotent.'

"But you said my amulet is fiction, meaningless superstition, how come you now feel your manhood threatened by it."

"I have experienced it, my manhood is…'

"So you are also unfaithful, you have tried it with another woman?"

"Yes, I have another woman; she's the one paying my fees here, she bought these clothes for me."

"Hmmmm, so that's it then?"

"What?"

"The unfaithfulness is mutual; I thought you only had me."

"Only two of you."

"That's one too many for me. Now get out of my room."

"What?"

"Get out, out."

And then a strange thought gripped Maimuna. What if she chased the reason for chasing men? What if rather than chase them for pleasure of sex, she now chased them for the pleasures of seeing them impotent. Her amulet would help her do this. Oh yes, she would not now go after men in search of what she had lost. No. She would now use her amulet to inaugurate a movement to make men impotent.

MAIMUNA'S BROTHEL OF MALE IMPOTENCE

Maimuna had been standing at the junction of Cornalus for three hours now waiting for the woman that would fulfil her yearning for a group of beautiful women representative of the twelve districts of her country. She already had eleven, the next woman would make it twelve- woman of national unity, like the new government.

But what about herself? Was she not a part of her women, her thirteenth woman? Thirteen, that jinx number of the western mind. Maimuna the thirteenth. No, she was not the thirteenth, she was the first. But was it not written that the first shall be the last. Maimuna ruminated over this, the first shall be the thirteenth - an odd number for an odd number. Maimuna the thirteenth. No. She stamped her left foot on the mud. Splashed on somebody. God! She had not been paying attention. That somebody the mud splashed on was the woman of her vision. Mud from her own feet all over the incarnation of the woman of her dream.

"I'm sorry dear, terribly sorry.'

'Ah me ah me," the woman replied, 'ah me."

Maimuna could see in the woman the effect of the fleeing road; the road pregnant with suffering and aborted hopes.

"I'm sorry em em... what's the name?

The woman told her

"From where?" she asked

She told her.

"Waw!" Maimuna could not hide her excitement at finally having a woman from the district she did not have a woman from. But she collected her excitement into a bag of remorse as her eyes met the new woman.

The new woman had the bashful looks of a woman who had once led the moral life, as defined by the holy men of her district. Her gaze was right, her gait tight.

"Where to?" Maimuna asked. She started walking her to the BMW bought her by her newest man.

"The camp" the new woman replied, 'the camp for displaced persons.'

"You've found it," Maimuna answered, "I'm the way to bliss, come into the car."

The new woman was confused, her upbringing cautioned her against strangers who acted too kind, especially so in big towns, especially so in Cornalus, one of the biggest of communities in the country. But she was also in dire need, and kindness is not something one who is in dire need throws away like that.

"Come in to the car," Maimuna repeated.

The new woman obeyed.

The new woman was a woman in pain, memories of forced wildness on a soul who was by nature and upbringing reserved. When the armed-renegades abducted her she had been set aside for the Commando. For that was their policy - all wondrously beautiful women for the Commando. After he had satisfied himself, he passed her on to the others down the line. First the men, the big men, then the little men, then kids, the boy-soldiers.

Maimuna eased into the driver's seat and drove away.

Into her place, a whole house she rented for her women. They called it the Wailing Places. And the soonest they entered it Maimuna announced.

"Sisters, I've brought another sister."

The Sisters swarmed upon the new sister; sighing a million concerns about her present and future. The new sister was overwhelmed. The questions The Sisters asked called for answers too intimate for the ears of strangers. For though they called her sister she still considered them strangers unto whom answers as to sex, heartaches and family secrets should not be divulged. But then The Sisters had long settled themselves into the necessity for these types of questions to every new woman in their midst. That way they hoped to do away with the historic tightness that has been woman's own in this part of the world.

How did they abduct you?
Where did they rape you?
Did you like any one of them?
Where guys from your village involved?
Do you know the guy who killed your father?
Have you ever had boyfriends?
Did you have sex with them?

The barrage continued until Maimuna brushed them aside, "sisters, I think we must let the new sister take her bath and change into some new clothes. Session time, remember, is just about thirty minutes away."

Then she turned to the new sister and said. "My sister, feel at home. You will enjoy your work here."

"What work?" the new sister asked.

"Well we heal men with wailing penises. We are having our regular session soon, but for you, it will be your initiation."

During the initiation, Maimuna's deputy spoke. She was wearing some sky blue boubou the cotton tree embroidered, the roots forming an arch half-way down the lambent gown, and inside that arch a flower, the petals five, white, the pollens blue... a silvery stalk, going down, dangling, almost touching the white high heels... Behind, just below the shoulder blades, is a diamond shaped split mid down betraying a blue and white lappa... Beauty on display, gloating eyes dancing to the music of her gait... She said, "this place, dear sister, is a clinic, and men are our patients. The sisters here are the nurses running the ambulance service to this place. We fish out the chronically ill men from the streets or nightclubs or offices and bring them here. We also administer first aid. First Aid treatment takes place anywhere - in homes, offices, clubs - depends on the man's erotic condition. After which Maimuna administers the ultimate therapy. We then come in to see whether the patient is responding to treatment. And, of course we don't do it for free; they pay for it, big money, we need the money to take care of ourselves and other women. We donate to women causes.

"College woman," Maimuna joked, "speaking like a real woman from college. But I think we need a lightening of your thick-talk." Maimuna called another sister to put it a plain simple language

Another sister came forward. She was wearing some heart-necked sleeveless mint green blouse, transparent, one could see the sweet tips of the firm breasts, succulent, and the fine hairs thinning out from some place thick with them underneath the tight fitting white trousers opening the beautiful sandals embracing, caressing, loving the baby soft feet… beauty beckoning phalluses almost tearing trousers. She explained, "dear sister, we make men impotent. We bring them to Maimuna who administers impotency to them."

"Come on,' another sister said to the new sister, "take this dress."

And the new woman put it on: topless, save for a honey-coloured tulle tied around the dancing breasts.... Black shorts barely covering the waist....Dreamy eyes white, brown, glassy, men beholding those eyes would see themselves in them. The eyes were mirroring. Men ogled at them; they leered at and saw themselves themselves reflected through those eyes, bulging with love, with emotion, wanting to possess, to aggress, to thrust phalluses, so irresistible...

THE EXPULSION OF LAMIN

Lamin did not mince his words as he stood before the disciplinary Committee of the College.

"I did not rape Maimuna; I only cut the amulet around her waist."

"And why did you do it?" The Chairman of the Committee asked.

'That I may be able to make love.'

"So you wanted to rape her but the amulet was preventing you from doing it?"

"No, I did not cut her amulet because I wanted to make love to her, but because I wanted to be potent for my out of campus woman."

"This boy is gone mad", another Committee Member said.

"Think so' replied another, "and I don't think this is a place for mad men."

"Sure," said another, "this is not a place for mad men."

Lamin went to his room; he was not going to wait for the Committee's letter to him. He already knew what would be in it; before his own eyes the Committee Members deliberated his expulsion: before his won eyes they pronounced him fit for the college's ultimate punishment. So why the hell should he wait for the letter of expulsion. He packed his things and zoomed out of college.

Two weeks later he published this long article that brought him into national limelight.

BLOOD-DANCE - By Lamin Forna

I want to talk here about circumcision, I mean female circumcision, or better still excision, Bundo, Sande, clitoridectomy, the cutting of the clitoris, of the mutilation or as its proponents would say, beautification of the female genitals.

Yes, I know this is a taboo topic, something that must not be publicly discussed - my belly may swell, God save me.

And God save the little girl waiting to be circumcised - to enter our culture's conception of the perfect woman - a woman who knows how to cook, how to sing, dance, plait, how to do home-chores, how to live with her man - she takes orders, must not refuse her man, especially when it comes to sex. But opponents say because the enjoyment of her sexuality might have been compromised by the cutting of that collection of sensitive nerves, because of the scarifications therein, she sees sex as a male endeavour, a male venture, so let him do all the work, all the sweating.

But all that is nonsense, say many proponent of Bundo, for can anyone tell us about any society without scarifications, without cutting? Must it be that it is cuttings of Africans by Africans that must savaged? What if the woman chooses to go through the cutting? Does

74

she not have the right to choose what to do with her body? And yes, many Bundo women say they still enjoy sex, they feel like full women. But opponents say there are many thousands who just lie still under the man, perhaps shifting here and there to ease the inconvenience of the man's weight, silently manipulating to get a better deal for herself in our androcentric society.

That she must learn how to live in a man's world that vital part of hers must be cut in unsanitary conditions, with unsterilised knives, a dance of oozing blood, the Sowei passes on to the next girl - the risk of transmitting diseases from one girl to the next is high. But what do the girls really learn? Especially when most Bundo now hardly last more than a few weeks.

Many older women bewail the worthlessness of this Bundo of short duration, which, anyway, seems to be the predominant one now, especially in the urban areas where now, due to rapid urbanisation, so many Bundo take place.

The older women say Bundo is not being done as tradition says it must. They shake their hoary heads at the trend of things: Bundo nowadays is not Bundo - the aura is not there, the moonlight revelry, the dance of sampa, the pageantry of ceremony, the beautiful mystery of the masked Bundo spirits, the sanctions, the discipline, the medicine have all been compromised. So now the girls come out before their sores heal, before learning the practised steps of womanhood; the rites are not properly done, the stench of childhood is never washed off the...

Hold your grumbling granny, Bundo can never be properly done in urban settings, for Bundo is a custom closely tied to the rural landscape, the rural ecology - the forest - Bundo bush, Bundo stream. But where can we get a Bundo bush here, or a stream clean enough to bathe the girls or forest to get the fresh herbs to heal the girls, or even space to teach our girls the exhilarating dancing steps of our rich heritage. The place is just too crowded. Lacks secrecy, the streams are dirt-dumps, too unclean.

Another point: this has to do with money, with material entitlements to Bundo elders to get them to forget about implementing certain disciplinary measures against girls who flaunt the rules, to get girls off certain hard and prolonged rites that were hitherto intrinsic part of Sande.

Hitherto Sande was an effective training institution. Despite all the mystery and secrecy it was a school, a socialising agent imbibing in girls skills necessary for better feminine existence in our patriarchal societies. Now, however, that role has been undermined. For instance, many Bundo must be rushed that the girls may return to school, to the formal educational institutions. And these institutions, wherever they are, in rural areas or urban centres, scoff at traditional knowledge producers like the sowei or digba. What teacher says at school is more important than what digba says.

Bur female circumcision is a complex issue, it is not an either/or affair.

Last year, a relative told me she was going to 'sunna' her six year old daughter. 'But she is too young,' I exclaimed.

"Yes," she affirmed, "even girls younger than her are being circumcised, it is less expensive... now that she has not yet known 'man business' she would not want expensive clothes and shoes when we get her out."

Make no folly about it, female circumcision is an expensive undertaking - costs millions. And what makes it harder is the tradition of extravagance that goes along with it. You have to provide far more than enough. The Bundo officials are always calling for more palm oil, rice, rum, this, that. Sometimes families that have circumcised their daughters find it very difficult to subsist come the rainy season. But tradition must have its fill, and people are ready to suffer all consequences to let it have its fill. It did not kill our mothers; so it will not kill our daughters.'

Except, as we are told, the witches amongst them. Witches they say, hardly survive the mystery ordeals of circumcision. The lesser witches are purged, but the daring ones don't have it easy. For Sande is also a screening mechanism - a process of purging girls of anti-traditional society, anti-woman practices like witchery, loud-mouth, arrogance, and licentiousness. It is believed that a woman with a clitoris has little control over her sexual urges. Cutting off the clitoris is a form of sex control (read: woman control).

Further insights: other times the death or illness of a girl in Bundo is attributed to other things - like the evil medicine of a rival sowei; or that the girl has eyes (clairvoyant) with which she sees things she must not see. Death or illness in Bundo is hardly blamed on the institution itself. Why should it be? Have you not heard people say 'the girl done go meresin' - the girl has gone to be healed. Bundo is a medicine, a healing, making a person whole and worthy before society. Before Bundo, a girl is not complete; she is ambiguous, somehow dangerous. Hence on initiation she's painted white, the ultimate colour of evil, sorcery and fear in our cultural chromatics.

This symbolic being must be brought low; the rites of washing away this whiteness symbolises the reclamation of this femme fatale, her redemption for service into community.

Something else! It is the use of the word 'sunna' to refer to female circumcision, especially the one done without drumming and dancing. Sunna, in Islam, means the practices of the Prophet Muhammad that Muslims must endeavour to imitate. No, female circumcision is

78

not a sunna, it is not an orthodox Islamic tradition - it is not incumbent on Muslims, it is non-existent in Islamic lands like Saudi Arabia and Iran.

And in Christianity also, circumcision of the flesh is insignificant. It is circumcision of the heart that makes individuals heirs of the promise.

But our preachers rarely talk about this persistent and pervasive feature of our culture. They are mute; it is a taboo topic, should not be talked about.

This brings to mind an interesting theory of muteness. A part of it says one way to deny the importance of a position is a refusal to engage in a discussion with it, with the other sides of Bundo, the ones that point to its shortcomings, its descent into meaninglessness.

All this relates to the dynamics of suppression and oppression and intolerance. Like when a younger person and an adult have some disagreement. The young one is not given sufficient hearing: it is suddenly hushed, so the adult wins. Like when a man wrongs his wife. The woman is not given sufficient hearing, the elders refuse to listen to the fine details of her story - so the man is always on top. The imposed silence of the woman gives the man voice, and he who has the voice carries the topic. The same with this Bundo talk. Shayma are the only people that...

But that there are other sides to it is a fact. Female circumcision exacerbates menstrual pains, increases the likelihood of infections and complicates childbirth.

But then these concerns are hardly given voice by the shayma or sandehnia. They've taken oaths of silence. But do they know that some or the persistent vaginal pains are the result of clitoridectomy? There is a growing perception in all segments of Sierra Leonean womanhood that something is amiss. Rituals, however die hard. Even where they have lost their relevance people cling to them for identitarian reasons. And where the effect of the ritual is irreversible, like in Bundo, it becomes internalised, an intrinsic part of a people, the scar becomes physical memory, a crest of ancestry that must be passed on to daughter.

So you see why the shayma or sandehnia, who are supposedly the victims of this tradition, are its ardent supporters, so you see why it is the gborrka or kpoway who feel comfortable enough to cry foul on behalf of our womanhood. But the sandehnia would not listen to the kpoway. It is part of her heritage to scorn the uninitiated adult. When it comes to Bundo the shayma must not heed even the most learned or most televised gborrka. What is cockroach (book addict) is a case of oozing blood.

Perhaps we should also hook this to the arrogant ignorance of Bundo opponents - this their way of holding their nose as they whisper about Bundo - like Bundo is some foul smelling thing. This makes those who have undergone circumcision come together in camaraderie of dignity against these incomplete women throwing mud of incomplete analysis at everyone. It has now become a cold war of mutual contempt. Supporters and opponents hardly dialogue.

So myths flowers, like when the uncircumcised say those circumcised have cannibalised their clitorises; like when the circumcised say the uncircumcised always carry lime to stop the itching of their uncut clitorises. Or like when they call those men (of country parentage) who oppose clitoridectomy cultural traitors, ingratiate children of circumcised women, potho, pumoi, black-white men who too much book has spoilt; or worthless dogs wallowing in the insatiable lust of an uncircumcised woman.

But not long ago I was with a woman, who now has a painful gait, unlike the gaiety and swaying joyfulness she had before she was circumcised hardly two months ago. Her once sparkling eyes now betray a memory of pain, a presence of dolour, a foretaste of the pain of giving birth. The Soso say ginehya-gonor -womanhood is painful. Nature or culture, or both, what is to blame?

THE SEPARATION OF LAMIN AND SATA

Reactions to Lamin's article ranged from the rowdy to the rude. Maimuna read the article and sent a scathing letter to Lamin accusing him of not acknowledging her as the inspiration for his new found views.

Lamin did not reply to Maimuna's letter; he had sworn to get out of her, and his foray into journalism was part of that effort. No, he would concentrate on his writing.

And concentrate on his work he did. His articles were much sought after. He wrote with nerve, with finesse, conviction. One day however an article he wrote about a businessman was rejected by all the papers; all the forty-something papers in the country. He was nonplussed. Why? The article had been thoroughly researched, wonderfully investigated. That businessman had been contracted by government to get furniture for about 500 newly built schools. Lamin's investigation revealed that the contractor bought furniture for less than a quarter of those schools. He had all the details, but editors refused to publish the article.

Later he learnt that all the country's editors were in the adverts list of that businessman. He gave them adverts all the time, on Independence Day, Eidul Fitri, Christmas, State Opening of Parliament, The Return of democracy,

The Clearance of a slum, adverts congratulating the President and others on their wonderful achievement.

Lamin, brimming with hurt, decided to set up his own newspaper. He called it 'The Rising Star'. He tried to get the money to set it up from his brother Koth Yaro. But Koth Yaro was not particularly keen on giving him the money. But Lamin's mother, also Koth Yaro's mother cried her eyes out imploring him to give Lamin the money.

Lamin launched into the paper ambitiously. He got ten people to staff his paper, all on salaries; something unheard of in the country's journalism. He wanted to give his staff salaries that would dissuade them from using their I.D. cards to squeeze money out of people. But no, his staff did many of the bad things the country's journalists were known for. The paper faltered. Even though sales were good, he could not recover the costs of production and salaries to staff. Adverts, the main avenue through which newspapers sustained themselves did not come his way. This was because his editorials lambasted almost all business concern. At first the business people thought he was only doing what they called ACD - Attack, Collect, Defend. You attacked the person in your paper, he was frightened; he called you aside to collect money, you collected; and now you defended him. But Lamin refused to collect; he refused to defend. So the adverts stopped coming.

He went to Sata for money to save his fledging newspaper. Sata told him, 'Lamin, I want you to drop out of this paper business and continue your schooling.'

'But how?' Lamin asked. 'I have been expelled from the only University in this country.'

'You could go to Ghana, Legon. I heard many guys expelled from the University here finished their degree courses there.'

"Yes, but some turned out to be the original brains behind the rebel mayhem in the country.'

'You would not be that, eh? I will give you the money. I will pay for everything, just check out what it takes.

When Sata gave Lamin the money to go to Legon he poured all of it into his newspaper; and lost it. He went to Sata again. Sata was so angry with him that he showed him the door.

Lamin was devastated. Why should Sata forsake him; it was for her sake that he cut Maimuna's amulet and was expelled from college. It pained him; every front now seemed bleak - his love affair was going under, his newspaper was in the red, his educational advancement had been halted.

About forty days after Sata showed him the door, he came around information implicating Sata and her husband, Mr. Sahr in a misappropriation racket. Lamin smiled wryly. Now this was an opportunity for patching up their relationship. He believed Sata would be grateful to him for the information he was going to give her. He would in the guise of cross checking the information forewarn her to take measures to forestall the adverse effects of the information leak of the unpleasant details of inflated costs and expenses.

For once Lamin was prepared to suspend his principles, to do what others were doing. No, this was a different case. No, the other did theirs for purely materialistic reasons; he was doing his for love. He wanted to be grateful. He owed Sata that. Sata had sacrificed too much for him; Sata had a child for him. Yakubu Chernor. Mr. Sahr still thought Yakuba was his child. Stupid man. Women say if you are told to sacrifice a stupid animal, look no further, it is a man, a husband, a human male in love.

But when he went to Sata with all these good intentions, she was angrier than ever before.

"Get out rapist," she shouted. "Now I know why you were expelled from college. Maimuna Kabba has told me. Get out, good for nothing rapist."

Lamin shouted back. It pained him that Sata could not appreciate the great sacrifice of principles he was making to divulge information to him. In his anger he called her what most men were wont to call successful women they disagreed with: prostitute; he called her that most abused word in the arsenal of male rudeness, -

prostitute. And he threatened to publish what he had on Mister Sahr and her.

"Go away, carry out your threat; publish everything you know, go, go, go!"

Lamin did go. And he did publish this article in his paper.

LUNCH FOR THE RECONSTRUCTIONISTS

A source close to THE COMMITTEE FOR THE RECONSTRUCTION OF THE PALACE OF THE PEOPLE has disclosed that the amount of money spent in providing lunch for committee members during committee meetings has outstripped the projected cost of the actual reconstruction.

The source also revealed that the contract for the provision of the lunch was given to the committee's chairman's wife, Sata Sahr (nee Thula), who is ill-qualified for it.

Futhermore, the source intimated this paper that the chairman, Mr. Fatorma Sahr, and cohorts are deliberately delaying the conclusion of their deliberations to enable the stingy wife who underpays her employees to reap as much money as possible from government.

KNICKERS OF MEMORIES

Koth Yaro studied botany at the University. It was there that he developed a taste for collecting and classifying things. He collected lots of stuff, but lately he was fixated on collecting and classifying knickers of ladies he had slept with. He spent his quiet moments sniffing the knickers; he enjoyed it, the scent of sex, smell was tied to his ability to remember stuff.

He labelled all the knickers - the owner, the time he got it from her, and the manner he got it. The one he was sniffing now had the label Maimuna; Feb. 97 10:p.m. Saturday. He enjoyed his time with her. He had told his friend Mister Sahr, "that woman was great." Mister Sahr requested, "link me up man." Koth Yaro replied, "No problem. The times are dawned upon us, we are all rivals now."

Koth Yaro put down Maimuna's knickers down and sniffed another. He looked up its label - Fanta: Feb 97 10:30p.m. Monday. Yes. Fanta, the beautiful woman for whom he could not become strong. He tried all the tricks in the books, she tried all the pranks in the trade, no success. He tried other women in an effort to disprove this disturbing discovery, no success. So with Mr. Sahr, he went to a medicine woman. The medicine-woman told him the reason for his impotence was that he made love unto someone that the taboos of his culture prohibited him from. Now he was suffering the consequences.

"What should I do now?" He had asked the woman.

"The Medicine is in your blood. But I doubt whether you would ever be completely healed. Tragedy, Koth Yaro, tragedy runs in the blood. Meanwhile, anytime you want to o make love you would have to rub your thing with soil from the grave of a virgin."

Koth Yaro was surprised at this temporary solution, but his friend Mister Sahr said he had been doing it and it worked. He said he had been doing a whole lot of stuff told him by the medicine woman and that he would attribute a large part of his wealth to doing what the woman told him to do.

Koth Yaro held these practices suspect. In his quieter moments he believed all this was nonsense. All this talk about witches and sorcerers and krifi, all were just part of the encompassing belief in the supernatural that was responsible for so much nonsense in the continent. A simple accident, they blamed it on the supernatural; a major accident, they blamed it on the supernatural; some one failed an exam, the supernatural; the chief fell ill, the supernatural; a man got impotent, the supernatural.

He was a man of science: the causes of male impotence, or erectile dysfunction have scientific explanations within the sub-branch of urology called

89

andrology. The literature says millions of men some of the time suffer from erectile dysfunction. Its pathophysiology suggests that penile erection is controlled by either reflex erection caused by touching the penis or psychogenic erection which has to do with emotional or erotic stimulation. When blood cannot enter the spongey bodies within the penis, the penis cannot become erect; or when the nerves in the penis cannot receive signals from the brain, the penis cannot become erect. These are no supernatural explanations requiring supernatural interventions. Perhaps Mr. Sahr and himself were having erectile dysfunction because they smoked a lot, or because they were getting fatter, or because of some hormonal deficiencies, or because the arteries in their bodies were becoming narrower as they aged. These could be the scientific explanations. He had only gone to the medicine woman because Mr. Sahr had insisted that they go.

Koth sniffed another knicker. Looked it up. Sia. Feb 97, Wednesday 11 p.m.. That too was an encounter of impotence. But why should he be pulling out only these memorabilia of pain. Had he not good times, swell hours?

He turned the collection of knickers upside down, like a fowl foraging for food. He took another knicker; looked it up: Maseray he looked no further. Maseray, the young girl he brought home from a night club one night

90

and for whom he kicked his first wife Yeanor out of the matrimonial bed.

Maseray, the woman with the cries that sent waves through nerves. Maseray, mother of the only child he ever fathered. That…. God, how easily memories change from the pleasurable to those that hurt?… that big headed boy. How shameful it was to be father of such a big headed boy. First glance at him and he straightaway wanted him dead. Afterwards the Maseray who perhaps could have made him love him had died giving birth to him, this son, this big headed boy.

But his younger brother, Lamin, was fond of this boy. Koth Yaro could not understand his younger brother. Unsteady head. He dropped out of college to become a journalist. Worthless occupation, nose-poking occupation, useless boy, aren't there other things to do? Why should he waste his brain telling the world about who messed up who? Useless boy.

But why should Sata, wife of his best friend Mr. Sahr, so love him? Why should Sata deny him and go along with this little Lamin? Why?

Koth Yaro remembered the time he tried to make love to Sata. "No", She replied, "You're my husband's best friend."

"But", Koth Yaro replied, "you have no qualms about making love to my brother, your husband's best friend's younger brother".

"All the more reason why I should not allow you. It's taboo to make love to two brothers... The consequences are grave."

Koth Yaro contemplated that statement - 'its taboo to make love to two brothers, the consequences are grave.' He turned it over and over in his mind.

LIFE AT THE EDGE OF THE LITTLE TOE

To stop thieves hooking out their belongings, Wara and Yembeh seal off the window that once allowed sunlight and moonlight in to their bedroom under the stair-cellar. So now the stair-cellar-bedroom-no-parlour is nearly always dark. And smelly damp: the latrine and wash-yard which is also the piss-yard are next door. And small: the bed's foot-side almost touches the doorpost. The pots and plates are all in the under-bed playground of roaches and rats. There are no chairs, no tables. And only one grown up can sleep there. For two to do that, one should be on top of the other, like in a conventional love-making posture. So only Wara sleeps there, bent like a bow to make room for her baby. Yembeh sleeps elsewhere.

Not that they have not tried to get a place where they can get pillow talks. But getting a place to do that in Cornalus is harder than getting a family. But what is a family without a place of their own. Father here, mother putting up with cousin there, one child upcountry with sister, two over the next street toting ice all day for Mami Ice for plate and place.

Sometimes when luck smiles and some space is won, it is so small that only sleeping, touching one another is possible. And for husbands and wives, rarayboys and

93

taptomi, that often results in unplanned love-making and birth of countless urchins cuddling at the foot of the bed.

And under-bed. With rats squeaking anytime mama and papa bed-dance in the dark. Life under-bed is full of stories about life in holes so great that sometimes the children follow the rat into their holes to know their whelps and the other marvels of rat-hood: like how to live in the dark without being noticed by mama and papa; like how to steal bread; go without bathing but without bad odour for months; eat books without learning; nimble soles like witches without stopping owners sleeping soundly...like mama and papa are doing now exhausted by their frenzied bed-dance.

But when heavy rain falls, as in August and September, and the rotten waterproof over the rustic zinc roof is swept away, and everywhere leaks so irritatingly, and mama and papa wake up, and the children rise up with their rat revelations, and cold everything rushes in from everywhere; it is not unknown for fathers to cuddle grown-up daughters for warmth, or sons to snuggle up to moms for heat, or for brothers and male cousins to seek warmth in the bobbling breasts of sisters and female cousins.

But now is not August, not September, and every-where is March hot... so hot that Wara sighs, 'ah dry season is bad hearted... sun spits in the rainy season but rain never comes in the dry season...'

A child wails. Wara darts into the dark stair cellar-bedroom-no-parlour and picks her up. She goes on howling… This child is truly sick, so angular, like a mangy rat.

Wara sings to her. Fondles. Caresses. Rocks. Swings.

The child howls. Moans. Gasps. Coughs. Gapes… So angular this child… like a mangy rat…Lamin appears, stands before Wara.

"Ah Lamin you come like some dream"

"Well if you wake up, I'll go." He is carrying a shoulder bag. In the bag are files. In one of the files is a packet. In the packet are A4 size papers. Seven of these papers are photocopies of sensitive documents relating to the Committee for the Reconstruction of the People's Palace.

"Come sit down," Wara offers him her seat.

"No, you sit… You are the one holding a child… Eee what is wrong with her?"

"Long time since your last visit"

"It's the job Wara… Man so busy."

"Everybody man blames his job…even Yembeh, that is what he says… the job the job the job… The job is like a witch, it has no lawyers… Busy busy busy even for his own child. He leaves everything to me even as sick as this child is… If they had killed her he would have been too busy to…

"Who wanted to kill your child?"

"Sorcerers, those who have eaten their own heart. They had already stabbed my child with their sorcerers' knives. Only that they had not yet spilled the blood to the ground. My child was weaker than jelly, weaker than jelly. I carried her to this doctor, nothing; that doctor nothing… God bless Mami Bura"

Lamin taps his head, "Mami Bura Bura Mami Bura who?"

"Ah Lamin, why are you behaving like a stranger? Has this your too much book book write write business made you forgot the old woman who…'

"Ah yes yes she warned Maseray not to wash in the open spaces of the night…"

"Yes that's her, but Maseray didn't heed her advice."

"It was good she didn't."

"Well that was why she gave birth to a krifi-child."

"Ah Wara that was just the tip of a story deep down intertwining with other stories. And some of these stories were good for you."

"What do you mean by 'some of these stories were good for me?'"

"Like the blindness of Pa Sorki, it lessened his power. And that blindness was caused by the krifi-child."

"And what has that got to do with me?"

"Well I heard people say that your marriage with Osman ended because the krifi-child destroyed Pa Sorki."

Yes she knows that. Pa Sorki was the greatest medicine-man Cornalus had known since its founding by Pa Alusine. And that he wanted her for his son Osman was an open secret. So yes, perhaps, had it not been for his blindness she would still be married to Osman, hooked up unto Osman by the spells of his father… Powerlessness engulfs Wara. Not that the bare facts of Lamin's account are strange to her, it is their overwhelming connection to the path of her life that astounds her. So Maseray's taking bath in the open spaces of the night had something to do with her life. But what if the pregnant Maseray had not washed in the open spaces of the night? How would she have fared with her life if Maseray had listened to the old woman's advice? This world is deep, very deep, and deep there, everything is connected to everything.

"Lamin, we are too connected to one another, too connected."

"Well, you may be right, although many times I doubt these connections. But that is our world. Sometimes I believe, sometimes I don't believe."

The Mangy-child moans. Wara thrust her breast into her tiny mouth.

"But you've not yet told me about your child and what Mami Bura did for her."

Wara begins this other story of her life!

"You see, helping people pays; goodness never falls on the ground. I often toted water for Mami Bura, went to market for her, washed her dirty clothes. She told me my child's sickness was not an illness for the hospital. She told me that if I did not stand up strong I would lose my child. I did not know about these things so I cried to her, "Please help me Mami Bura, give birth to me, take me like your own, help me." She led me to a medicine-woman. The medicine-woman gave my dying child this drink and that, that and this... whispered this to herself then to my child, this and that... Then she started rubbing my child with her fingers, feeling for her life, pinching her fingers, rubbing this murmuring that... She was getting tired, my child was dying. It was passed midnight...

"Go out," the medicine-woman suddenly ordered me, "cuss them... cuss their fathers, their mothers, all their family, cusses weaken the powers of sorcerers, go cuss them, that will help weaken their hold on the little pikin."

I rushed out and blasted all bad people. After about an hour of cussing in the middle of the night, Mami Bura called me, 'come in now, your child is getting better.

I couldn't believe my eyes. I met my child crying, my child who had not even opened her eyes for over a week crying very loud, hot steaming vomit all over her.

"Suckle her," the medicine woman ordered. "She's a lucky child. Her life was almost gone, already at the edge of the little toe... I pinched it back into her body... she will have a long life."

"Did she tell you their names," Lamin asked Wara.

"Who?"

"The sorcerers."

"Watch under your foot; if a relative does not open the door, the sorcerer will not enter."

"And who is this relative?"

"He came here, Pa Kaly, my own father and confessed.'

'Unbelievable!'

Wara continued her story:

"I was surprised to see my father. He had taken an oath that he would never visit me. What then could be the reason for this visit? But I did not have long to wait. Father was fast on his belly, holding my feet.

"Please Wara don't disgrace me, I did it for you. It's a long story. I owed a debt on account of you... But since I couldn't pay them with your life, I had to pay your child."

"Forgive him'. It was Ya Sento, my mother. "I have forgiven him..."

"Eee Mama." I was really taken aback. It was like I was dreaming. I held father and helped him up. I looked him in the eyes and suddenly all the hate I had borne for him vanished. I saw

99

love in his eyes. How is it that ways of showing love sometimes create so much pain for both lover and loved. Tears welled up in my eyes; I fell on the ground, prostrate, "Father, forgive me."

"That was how it happened, Lamin. I have some rice... let me get some for you?"

"I've just eaten."

Rain falls even on rivers... Hold this child let me get some rice for you."

"Okay Okay, but before you go bring food, please hide these papers for me. They are very sensitive... and I suspect they want to raid my place for them."

When Wara returns with the food, Lamin asks her, "will this girl be circumcised?"

"Why do you ask?"

"I hate it, I hate to see girls circumcised."

"Hmm school has spoilt you!"

"It's painful, barbaric..."

"It didn't kill me; it will not kill her."

"It's bad, it makes..."

"But you were circumcised."

"I'm a man."

"So only men should be circumcised. Women are not good enough to become real people."

"If God gives me a daughter, she will not be circumcised."

"You will have to kill your mother first"

"My daughter is my child, my own child and…"

"Her grandchild… You have scored a goal against yourself. Now eat, you who too much book has spoilt."

KOTH YARO AND MR. SAHR

Koth Yaro and Mr. Sahr are best of friends. Like teeth and tongue, they are always together. But since the imprisonment of Lamin for writing a newspaper article against Mr. Sahr and his wife, Sata, the relationship has not been that good.

Koth Yaro wants his brother out. Lamin's mother, also Koth Yaro's mother, is dying out of grief for Lamin. This is tormenting Koth Yaro. And worse, everyone is blaming him for not doing enough about it. They say he does not love Lamin, that he has always wanted him down. But God knows this is false. He loves Lamin as he loves his own spinal cord. But Lamin is stubborn, very adamant. How many times has he not warned him to moderate his stance? How many times has he not told him to drop this profession of poking nose into other people's business and find some better things to do. He even gave him some money to do that. But what did he do with it? He bought contraband newsprint with it. And he was the one who saw this and that to get him out of trouble. No one bothered to do anything about it, not one of the masses whom he boasted to be fighting for, stirred.

And now, look at him here today, alone, begging Mr. Sahr for the umpteenth time to let his brother go. But

Mr. Sahr is insisting that he should talk to his wife. "I would have got him out but Sata wouldn't hear about that, all now depends on her, she received the greatest insults... Talk to her."

Mr. Sahr calls out to his wife, "my dear, Koth Yaro wants Lamin out but I told him everything depends on you."

"Let him stay there for few more days, that will put him in his place."

"What!" Koth Yaro knows that Lamin and Sata are lovers; he does not believe his ears.

"She is hurt the most," Mr. Sahr continues, "she he called ill-qualified."

"Because I didn't go to college...well let his college get him out."

"What!"

"She is hurt the most, she he called dry-hearted...stingy."

"Because I refused to give in to him... He came here and told me about what he wanted o write; I showed him the door."

"What!"

"Yes, so he insulted her, called her a prostitute, a call-girl of Kapay Jahanama."

"I blame myself, not him. He is a rapist. That was why he was expelled. He raped my cousin, my own cousin, Maimuna. Let him stay there,..."

"Maimuna! Is Maimuna your cousin?" Mr. Sahr is nonplussed

"Yes Maimuna Kabba, my own cousin, her late mother was my mother's eldest sister. Let him stay there, bastard dog let him stay there…" She rushes out flapping her hands on her hips, slapping her temples.

"Maimuna!" Mr. Sahr stares.

"Maimuna!" Koth Yaro gapes.

"Hmmm!"

"Hmmm!"

Koth Yaro clearly remembers his very first meeting with Maimuna:

He was in a shop buying some birthday presents for one of his girlfriends. Maimuna entered. White baseball cap, black T shirt, white waist coat, sporty black-white bag, black shorts, white sport shoes. She swanked to the counter, swung round, like she was dancing to some music. He involuntarily smiled. She smiled back. This should mean something. He went up to her and offered his hand. She ignored it. His heart sank. She smiled, rolled over her eyes, leaned on the counter, dangled her foot, and said, "You have the eyes and nose of the only man I love. But he has walked out of my life." "I'll never do it." "Only he knows how to, no other man will ever walk out of my life again." When Maimuna finished shopping, Koth Yaro offered to drive her home. "Where do you stay?" "College," she answered, "I'm a student." "Do you know Lamin? He's my younger brother." "No I don't know him."

"He's very popular, a student activist." "I hate popular people,"
she replied, "they're cheap. I wish all popular people were
impotent."

Koth gets out of reminiscing and says to Mr. Sahr,
"Maybe Maimuna is the cause of our impotence."
"Maybe!"
"Maybe"
"She castrates men with her amulet, takes away their
power. No wonder Lamin raped her, may be it was to
free himself from her curse!"
"Perhaps."
"Then I must get him out…what's the time'
"Nine"
"It's late now."
"Tomorrow."
"It's cleaning Saturday, nothing is done on cleaning
Saturdays."
"Monday then."
"Yes, Monday."

THE DEATH OF MAIMUNA

Maimuna is the tallest desperado in the open field in the raging storm... the brightest...dreaming the grand idea about building strong houses against the howling storm... strong houses that do not leak, that do not let in the gusty cold of the whirl-rain.

The brothel where they were, where all were rivals unto one another, that building was collapsing on their heads. So they ran into the open field on the way to the dream house on the other side. That house leaks not, it is homely... Even from a million miles you could see the happy luminance of its inhabitants, so happy, obviously oblivious of the raging storm.

That's the house they are running to and Maimuna is the tallest being, so brilliant, understands the language of the inhabitants of the house across the field...the tallest mortal in the open field in the thunderstorm...gba gba gba...

Some time back, before it became a brothel, the vacated house was not very good enough, was not perfect, the rafters did not let in rains, irritating droplets, did let in gusts of wind, but huddled together in the little space where no water dropped was warmth enough.... Joy!

106

But now it leaks everywhere, all over...through the eaves and the myths and stories and proverbs stuffed here and there to keep out the frigid questions of existence... The spirits are adamant that lately, all are rivals in that house, that holy is unholy, that the men are rapists, the women are prostitutes. So now it leaks as if there are no thatches and the croaking questions, millions, louder that the rhythmic drumming which had hitherto pushed them off the lobes of the inner ears.

That is warning enough... for those who hearken... So they run out, led by this brave woman, they dare the raging storm.

But the fools stay behind... they will not abandon the tombs of their ancestors. What magnanimous reciprocity! And they say; we will give birth to our lifeless parents. So they go into their women with a new resolve, a new savage hardness. What cruel magnanimity.

But she ventures out, without her amulet that had been cut by Lamin. She ventures out, holding on high a bamboo obelisk bloody phallus-like, perchance this memento may be needed in the dream house across the open field in the raging storm palalala lala...

But she is an amazon, fearless, she wears no shoe, has no amulet, only a cummerbund, does not even know it, her head is upon the dream house across the field- a house so strong, leaks nowhere, no reason to snuggle up to one another for warmth. The house lets in no gusts of biting wind, human warmth is superfluous, you can be warm without touching another. The other is superfluous.

But in a flash of lightening she reads, she sees, she remembers; some people from the vacated house helped built that house... strong people; kidnapped by knighted saints; kicked out by their own drunken people... What many corpses beneath this watery field what many bones under that sandy esplanade! What alliance of evil people, over there, over where they were, are, rules this world.

But she is the tallest, the brightest, and she holds on the memories of the oppression, the story of a bloody phallocracy, the obelisks of a violent patriarchy that normalised the beating of women and the throwing out of their things. And she has no shoe on, her head is on the dream: the new earth must be a better place for all, for all.

So the thunder hails her and...hails down on her...!

Behold the way, the wayfarer and the wayfaring rest in God!

Behold the dream home has vanished, gone with the head!

So there we are, the migrants, confused, nude now, no kerchief over our scalps, no raiment on our souls, mercilessly beaten by the hail, by the wind, no shelter yet, nothing, no dreaming, no dream head with a way to the dream house.

YEMBEH RECOLLECTS

"Yes. Lamin is dead. He was shot yesterday. And I'm a party to it... I don't know why... I must tell Sata, tell Wara, tell all that Lamin is no more. I must tell them that Kapay Jahanama had a bad fit and shouted, "men oh men let's go for those Lumpa guys; long time since I last shot and killed..."

I must tell Sata and Wara that like soldiers we had jumped to the command and rushed to the Central prisons. That we called out the Lumpa people. That Lamin came out too, "I too must be freed, I must be, I did nothing wrong." That some of us know had tried to push him off with twisting mouths and blinking eyes. That he had stubbornly refused. That Kapay Jahanama ordered us to fling them all in to the truck, like bags of palm kernel. That we carried them to the edge of town, to the forested hills beyond Funkia. I must tell them no bullet could go inside Lamin. That we had to flog him with cassava stems, then hit him with sticks, then tie this foot to this jeep, that to the other truck and drove apart. That we dumped them inside one mass grave and poured acid upon them... I must tell Sata, must tell Wara... But how? How? That I was... that Kapay Jahanama had... that I come all the way from the war with false papers to... I wish I had not come.... Horrible deaths at the war front, yes; but this, this my own friend, my own brother, confidante.… When I was about to be enlisted in the army I told him, soliciting his support, but he asked:

"Yembeh, why do you want to join the army?"

"Lamin, that is the only way left for me to be somebody that these foolish people in this foolish Cornalus can respect. Don't you see how they are treating me, how they've taken Wara away from me? Isn't it because I have no money, no power. Lamin I'm joining the army to be somebody…"

What heavy price to pay to be somebody. I wish I am dead, wish I was killed up there at the front, just like what many in Cornalus believed. But I did not die; rather I came down from the warfront, cowardly, with forged papers Sata sent me.

I became a member of Kapay Jahanama's most feared K Squad. I became a man and took my revenge on Osman. I shot him. It was right that I broke his foot. When he had power in the previous regime, he got a magistrate to throw my mother into prison. He wanted me, but I ran away; so they took my mother and threw her into prison; until my family had to grovel on their belly to beg his family to let my mother go. Then they called the magistrate, the selfsame magistrate who refused Lamin bail, the self same magistrate who Mr. Sahr bribed to get Lamin to prison for publishing Lunch for the Reconstructionists

"It was not for that alone," said Wara

"What else Wara, what else?" I asked her.

"He cussed Sata publicly, he called her a prostitute. He said Sata slept with Kapay Jahanama to keep her contract with the Committee For The Reconstruction of the People's Palace.

"But isn't that the truth… Kapay Jahanama himself told me about it, boastfully. I wasn't convinced; so Kapay made me hide in his wardrobe the other time round… And I saw them with my own eyes."

"And you told Lamin, You told him!"

"He's my friend… and it's the truth."

"Must we tell truths that hurt?"

"But must she tell her husband to jail Lamin."

"She loved Lamin, loves him still. She was going to get him out, she only did that to teach him a lesson. She was hurt, vexed, she had no other choice…"

"No other choice? There is always another choice. When I told Lamin that I wanted to join the army to become a man, he told me that there were many other ways to become a man.'

"True," said Wara, "there were many other things you could have done besides joining the army, many other things, but you chose it eh, you chose it…"

Yes, there are many other things I could have done besides joining the army, but I chose it. I chose to follow Kapay Jahanama into the prison yard. I chose to participate in the murder of my friend. But oh yes that same Magistrate who jailed my mother sent him there. He chose to do it. He chose it. I'll kill him, shoot him, break his leg. I'll kill him. Kill him.... No, Wara don't come into this, I know you will want to come into this... But no, I'll kill him, break his foot, his neck.

"There are many other things you could do besides killing him"

"Yes, yes Wara, but I must choose this... I must do this."

"Kapay Jahanama killed him, not the magistrate, go then for Kapay Jahanama."

"But it was the Judge who sent him there."

"But who sent him to the Judge. Sure, he didn't pick him out of the street like that. You know who did that..."

Yes, I know who sent him there. Mr. Sahr did it. Mr. Sahr, Mr. Sahr, Mr. Sahr. But why did Koth Yaro not intervene. Why Why Why? Mr. Sahr is his best friend, they are always together, even this very morning I saw them going into the law courts. But why must Koth Yaro always be with the man who jailed his brother? Why? For money? Because Mr. Sahr is rich? Oh yes money is thicker than blood. For money, Koth Yaro buzzes, like a fly, the arse of the man who jailed his brother. But what profit will it bring him, what profit?

"But it was Sata who asked Koth Yaro to ask the magistrate to send Lamin to jail."

And Yembeh suddenly laughed. He remembered stuff that made him laugh at what had happened. He remembered the days he spent with Wara hearing grown-ups groan. He remembered the funny drawings of Wara, the drawings that got her into trouble. But how they laughed afterwards watching the drawings and owning the drawings and owning what they imagine about people. He imagined a hundred and million things that kept him laughing

Why kill ourselves… so funny
Why are we afraid to kill… so funny
Why should I not kill the funny bastards…. So funny
I will kill him… so funny
Me and Wara…. We will laugh at the way Lamin died.
At the way his murderers shall die.
At ourselves killing.
And living. And laughing. And dying. And and and.

SIERRA LEONEAN WRITERS SERIES (SLWS)

Focusing on academic, fictional, and scientific writing that will complement other relevant materials used in schools, colleges, universities and other tertiary institutions, the Sierra Leonean Writers Series (SLWS) aims to promote good quality books by Sierra Leoneans writing on any topics and other writers from around the world who write on themes and issues about Sierra Leone.

It is the publisher's hope that students and other readers in Sierra Leone will eventually be at least some of the primary beneficiaries of these works. Not only will people in Sierra Leone be able to read materials that relate to their own lives and experiences, budding writers will also be able to draw inspiration from the efforts of their compatriots and other established writers.

Submitted work undergoes a rigorous peer-review process before being accepted for publication, with an international editorial board providing guidance to writers.

SLWS, based in Warima and Freetown in Sierra Leone, distributes books globally through AMAZON.COM. In Sierra Leone, SLWS books are currently available at the SLWS Bookshop in Warima (near Masiaka) and at CLC Bookshop, 92 Pademba Road in Freetown.

SLWS co-publishes some titles with Karantha Publishers in Sierra Leone.

For further information, please visit our website:
www.sl-writers-series.org
or contact the publisher, Prof. Osman A. Sankoh (Mallam O.)
publisher@sl-writers-series.org

Published Books – a milestone of the 50th title has been reached in September 2016!

1	Osman A. Sankoh (Mallam O.)	2001/ 2016	*A Memoir*	*Hybrid Eyes – An African in Europe*
2	Osman A. Sankoh (Mallam O.)	2001	*Non-fiction*	*Beautiful Colours*
3	Sheikh Umarr Kamarah	2002/ 2015	*Poems*	*Singing in Exile and The Child of War*
4	Abdul B. Kamara	2003/ 2015	*A Memoir*	*Unknown Destination*
5	Samuel Hinton	2003	*Poems*	*The Road to Kenema*
6	Karamoh Kabba	2005/ 2016	*A Novel*	*Morquee – The Political Drama of Wish over Wisdom*
7	Yema Lucilda Hunter	2007	*A Novel*	*Redemption Song*
8	Joe A. D. Alie	2007/ 2015	*Research Text*	*Sierra Leone Since Independence – History of a Postcolonial State*
9	Mohamed Combo Kamanda	2007	*A Play*	*The Visa*
10	J Sorie Conteh	2007	*A Novel*	*In Search of Sons*
11	Michael Fayia Kallon	2010/ 2015	*A Novel*	*The Ghosts of Ngaingah*
12	J Sorie Conteh	2011	*A Novel*	*Family Affairs*

13	Winston Forde	2011	*A Play*	*Layila, Kakatua wan bi Lida*
14	Eustace Palmer Doc P.	2012	*A Novel*	*A Pillar of the Community*
15	Siaka Kroma	2012	*Non-fiction*	*Manners Maketh Man – Adventures of a Bo School Boy*
16	Mohamed Combo Kamanda (ed)	2012	*Short Stories*	*The Price and other Short Stories from Sierra Leone*
17	Sigismond Tucker	2013	*A Memoir*	*From the Land of Diamonds to the Isle of Spice*
18	Bailah Leigh	2013	*Non-fiction*	*Dilemma of Freedom – A Diary from Behind Rebels Lines in the Sierra Leone Civil War*
19	Nnamdi Carew	2013	*A Novella*	*Tiger Fist – Two Stories*
20	Yema Lucilda Hunter	2013	*A Novel*	*Joy Came in the Morning*
21	Ebenezer 'Solo' Collier	2013	*Research Text*	*Primary & Secondary Education in Sierra Leone – Evaluation of more than 50 years of PRACTICES & POLICIES*
22	Gbananom Hallowell	2013	*Short Stories*	*Gbomgbosoro - Two Stories*
23	Sheikh Umarr Kamarah &	2013	*Poems*	**beg sol noba kuk sup** *- An Anthology*

	Majorie Jones (eds)			of Krio Poetry
24	Siaka Kroma	2014	Short Stories	Tales from the Fireside
25	Syl Cheney-Coker*	2014	Poems	The Road to Jamaica
26	Dr Sama Banya	2015	A Memoir	Looking Back – My Life and Times
27	Andrew K Keili	2015	Social Commentary	Ponder My Thoughts – Vol. 1
28	Jedidah A. O. Johnson	2015	A Novel	Youthful Yearnings
29	Oumar Farouk Sesay	2015	A Novel	Landscape of Memories
30	Oumar Farouk Sesay	2015	Poems	The Edge of a Cry
31	Gbanabom Hallowell	2015	A Novel	The Road to Kaibara
32	Mohamed Gibril Sesay*	2015	A Novel	This Side of Nothingness
33	Yema Lucilda Hunter	2015	A Novel	Nanna
34	Yusuf Bangura	2015	Research Text	Development, Democracy & Cohesion
35	Lansana Gberie	2015	Research Text	War, Politics & Justice in West Africa
36	Yema Lucilda Hunter	2015	A Biography	An African Treasure: In Search of Gladys Casely-Hayford 1904-1950
37	Moses Kainwo	2015	Poems	Ayo Ayo Ayo and other Love Songs

38	Abdulai Walon-Jalloh	2015	*Poems*	*Voices and Passions*
39	Gbanabom Hallowell (Ed.)	2016	*Short Stories*	*In the Belly of the Lion – An Anthology of new Sierra Leonean Short Stories*
40	Ahmed Koroma	2016	*Poems*	*Along the Odokoko River - Poems*
41	George Coleridge-Taylor	2016	*A Memoir*	*Transformation in Transition*
42	Karamoh Kabba	2016	*Research Text*	*Fire from Timbuktu: A Dialogue with History*
43	Umu Kultumie Tejan-Jalloh	2016	*A Memoir*	*Telling It As It Was: The Career of A Sierra Leonean Woman in Public Service*
44	Ambrose Massaquoi	2016	*Poems*	*Along the Peal of Drums: Collected Poems (1990-2015)*
45	Mohamed Gibril Sesay	2016	*Poems*	*At the Gathering of Roads (Poems)*
46	Gbanabom Hallowell	2016	*Poems*	*Manscape in the Sierra: New and Collected Poems 1991-2011*
47	Gbanabom Hallowell (Ed.)	2016	*Short Stories and Poems*	*Leoneanthology: Comtemporary Short Stories and Poems from Sierra Leone*
48	Gbanabom Hallowell	2016	*Poems*	*Don't Call Me Elvis and Other Poems*

| 49 | Bakar Mansaray | 2016 | *Short Stories* | *A Suitcase Full of Dried Fish and Other Stories* |
| 50 | Gbanabom Hallowell | 2016 | *Poems* | *The Art of the Lonely Wanderer* |

*co-published with Karantha Publishers